the Drag Race

debutante

and the

detectives

THE DRAG RACE DEBUTANTE AND THE DETECTIVES

ISBN: 978-0-6455781-9-5

Copyright © 2025 by Jennie Kew
Published by Wooden Key Press
Edited by Wooden Key Press
Cover by Mayhem Cover Creations

www.jenniekew.com

"...Toby was my perfect book boyfriend."
Review for *His Own Heaven*

"Their story is heartfelt, sweet, deliciously
hot and sexy, romantic and more."
Review for *The Viking Blues*

"It joins the rest of the series on
my keeper shelf."
Review for *Size Doesn't Matter*

"...funny and sexy, sassy and entertaining."
Review for *The Book Shop Girl
and The Billionaire*

"...very funny but also serious and heartfelt."
Review for *The Roller Derby Darling
and The Delinquent*

Foreword

While all efforts have been made to research police procedures in the Australian state of Queensland, please remember this book is a work of fiction and gross liberties have been taken in the name of creative licence.

For Mysty,
My favourite hoon.

The puzzle of three:
strong, connected, unwavering.
Albert Einstein

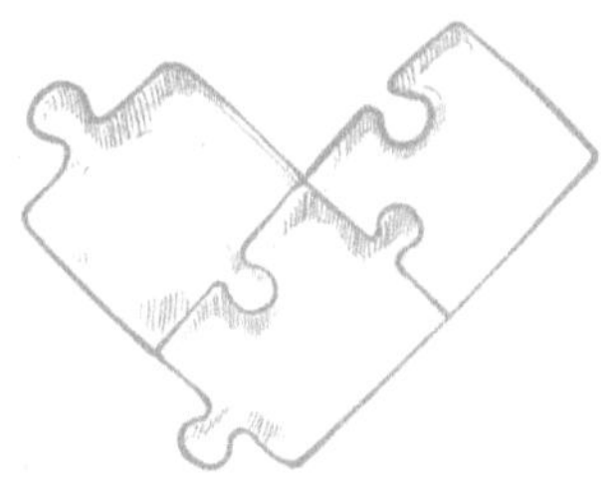

Chapter One

"What in the actual fuck?"

"We good?" Eric Walker responded quietly and calmly, knowing his younger brother would hear him through the listening devices they wore, despite the chatter of the crowd or the rumbling of engines.

"No, we are not," Dane replied, then sighed heavily. "You need to get over here. Now. We have a situation."

"Shit. Where are you?"

"Neon green Subaru, north of your position."

Eric turned and saw the neon coloured monstrosity, then did a double-take when a familiar brunette smiled and waved at him. "Fuck," he ground out between gritted teeth. "I'm on my way."

Eric made his way through the crowd, his bad mood worsening with every step. Of all the places to be on a Friday night, what the fuck was she doing *here*? Did her parents know what she was getting up to while they were away?

More to the point, did her brother?

"Convict will fucking kill us for this," he murmured, stopping beside Dane as the pair of them scowled at Emily Berringer, their future brother-in-law's little sister.

They'd met Emily a little over a year ago, at a roller derby event their sister was competing in, and upon seeing her bright smile, expressive eyes and curvy body, it had taken them approximately 0.3 seconds to fall head over heels in lust with her. As the older brother, Eric had quickly called dibs on her, a childish act that Dane had ignored just as fast. Then they'd sat on either side of her and flirted hard, causing her to smile and blush and tuck her long, dark hair behind her ears.

She was cute as fuck.

But then Edward 'Teddy' Berringer, the convict who thought he was good enough to marry *their* little sister had ruined their fun, his constant stream of questions about the rules of roller derby causing Emily to switch seats with Easton, the youngest Berringer sibling, and placing her out of their reach.

Since then, they'd bumped into Emily in a variety of places. Family barbeques, the book shop their sister managed, the car dealership her father owned, and the vintage auto garage her older brother ran. In the year since meeting her, they'd made the effort to get to know her as well as people could know each other with their clothes still on, even stealing kisses from her here and there— sometimes a little *more* than kisses—and rejoicing in the fact she seemed to enjoy their attention as much as they liked hers.

And somewhere in amongst all of that, Eric and Dane had made the decision that one way or another, Emily Berringer was going to be theirs. A simple goal that had become much more difficult since their secondment to the joint task force in charge of this shit show. And now she was here.

At an illegal street race.

The very *last* place she should be.

Eric folded his arms across his chest and stared down at her. "What are you doing here?"

Emily's smile faded at his harsh tone, and she mimicked his stance, folding her arms across her chest and drawing his attention to the distracting view of her ample cleavage. "And hello to you too, hot stuff."

His mouth twitched with both irritation and the urge to smile. One of the many things this woman excelled at—and one he appreciated more than he wanted to admit—was her sass. The smile won out, and Eric sighed in defeat. "Hello, Emily. But seriously, what are you doing here?"

She pursed her lips and tapped one perfectly manicured fingernail against her chin as she pretended to mull over her answer, then pointed a finger pistol at him and said, "Babysitting."

Dane chuckled and shook his head. "Babysitting? That's the best excuse you could come up with?"

She gave a one-sided shrug and looked away. "I wasn't sure you'd like the real answer, and at this point I'm not sure I care. Besides, I didn't know you'd be here."

Eric looked at Dane, then they both turned their best interrogation stares on her. "And what exactly is the *real* answer?"

Emily shifted her feet and fidgeted with the ends of her hair. She was nervous. She half shrugged again and refused to meet their eyes. "I might be here... on a date."

Eric's jaw tightened and the bottom fell out of his gut. "You're on a date?" he snarled.

"Who with?" Dane stepped closer, grabbed Emily's

hips and crowded her from behind, practically sandwiching her between them.

The feel of her soft body, her thighs, her stomach, her breasts pressed fully against Eric made his cock jump to attention and his hands itch with the need to touch her, to pull her even closer. He slid one hand into her loose hair and made a fist at the base of her skull, then slid his other hand around her throat, holding her with just enough force to let her know exactly how much trouble she was in.

"And whose idea was it to bring you to an illegal drag race?"

She swallowed, her throat moving against his palm. "I didn't know it was illegal," she said, her words punctuated by the revving of an engine. "He told me we were going to watch the supercars. I thought he meant at the Raceway in Willowbank." She gritted her teeth. "Obviously I was wrong."

"That doesn't explain why you're here with someone else."

"Or where this Romeo is," Dane added, looking around them.

Emily shot Eric a furious look, and he didn't doubt for one second she would have scowled at both him and Dane if she'd been able, but he held her fast, focussed all of her attention on him alone. "He went to find his brother," she snapped. "And why shouldn't I be here with someone else? It's not as if we're dating. And how am I the one at fault here when you two have made it perfectly clear you're no longer interested?"

Eric's brow scrunched as he continued staring down at her. "What do you mean 'no longer interested'?"

Dane wedged her tighter between them. "Does this feel like we're not interested?"

Emily rolled her eyes. "Wow. Is that a gear shift in your pocket or are you just happy to see me?"

Eric smirked at her dry tone and Dane shrugged. "Hey, you try being pressed up against this sweet arse and not getting hard."

A blush bloomed on Emily's cheeks and she squirmed between them, making his brother groan. As crass as Dane's comment was, she clearly enjoyed his attention. But what Eric didn't enjoy was her thinking they weren't interested in her anymore. Enough that she'd gone on a date with someone else.

Fuck.

And even though they had much more important things to discuss—like taking Emily home so she was nowhere near the illegal drag racing and drug deals they'd been tasked with investigating—he was finding it difficult to think about anything other than her warmth pressed against him, especially while she was wearing skin-tight jeans and a curve-hugging T-shirt that showed off every inch of her delectable body. Including a strip of bare flesh between said jeans and T-shirt that begged for his caress.

Closing his eyes, he took a breath and refocussed his attention to where it was needed. "I feel like we've gotten off track here." He stared at her again, a frown pinching his brow. "So, I will ask you one more time. Whose idea was it to come here tonight? Give me his name."

Lifting her chin, she glared up at him, her eyes sparking with bright blue fire. *Stubborn kitten.* "Dane, will you please tell Robo—"

Eric slammed his mouth down on hers. He told himself it was just to ensure her silence, to make sure she didn't utter the word 'cop' within earshot of the two drug dealers they'd already clocked, and blow their cover. But the longer he felt her soft lips under his, the more he wanted to kiss her properly, wanted to taste her, to feel her tongue lash against his. Wanted to run his fingertips over that bare patch of flesh at her waist and drown himself in her sweet scent.

Slipping his hand free from her throat, he slid it down her body, brushed the side of her breast, her ribs, felt her softness give under his possessive touch. And when he reached that sexy little strip of naked skin, he slid his hand to the small of her back and tugged her close, let her feel the evidence of how interested he truly was. Pressed his aching cock against her belly and swallowed her needy little moan.

It only took a moment for Emily to soften in his grasp, to wrap her arms around his back and scrunch her hands in his shirt, press her breasts against his chest. She gave him permission to push for more. So he did. He crushed her against him and kissed the ever-loving fuck out of her.

"That's our girl," Dane murmured against her neck.

When Eric finally eased back, he whispered against her lips, "Don't say the C-word, don't call us by name, and whatever you hear us say from here on out, just go with it. Do you understand?" Then he pulled back so he could stare down at her, ensure she did indeed understand his meaning.

Intelligent woman that she was, Emily's eyes widened and her mouth fell open on a gasp, then quickly snapped shut again. Her gaze darted around them, took in the various groups of people surrounding them, the money and the booze and the drugs they openly passed to one another, and she swallowed hard. When she looked back at him, he recognised the undercurrent of fear he saw in her eyes, the realisation of the danger she had put herself in by being there. And he hated that he and Dane and their carelessness were the cause of her recklessness.

"Oh. I see." She nodded, the fear dissipating from her

gaze as quickly as it had appeared, replaced by a glint of determination. "Understood."

Eric released the breath he didn't realise he'd been holding and relaxed his grip on her, shifting his hands to her shoulders and gently rubbing them. "Good girl. Now, we obviously have a lot to talk about, but now is not the time and here is not the place. We're taking you home."

Emily moistened her lips. "But don't you have to,"—she looked around them again—"you know? Do your thing?"

"Your safety is more important," Dane said, then looked over her head at Eric. "Let's get her out of here."

"Agreed," Eric said, then wrapped an arm around Emily's waist and turned her towards where their car was parked.

"Emily?" All three of them turned back to face a very confused looking young man carrying an open bottle of beer. "What the fuck?"

Emily stiffened in his embrace. "Oh. Matthew.... Hi."

Chapter Two

D ane stared at the beer carrying deadbeat before them and sniffed, unimpressed. "Is this the little twat who brought you here?"

He'd recognised the kid instantly as Matthew Spencer, the younger brother of the sadistic fuck in charge of the drag races, but he couldn't acknowledge that fact without tipping their hand. Undercover work was not his and Eric's usual purview, but they'd been tapped by their boss to lend a hand to the investigation, their in-depth knowledge of engines and their passion for racing cars in their free time making them ideal candidates for the job.

Personally, Dane couldn't wait to get back to their usual job of everyday policing. The Walker family had been Queensland police officers for four generations, and he and his brother were proud to wear the blues and continue that tradition. Undercover work required a certain amount of deceit that didn't sit well with either of them. Especially when it meant deceiving the people closest to them, and distancing themselves from the one person they'd hoped to become *very* close to.

Even if it had been unintentional.

"Seems like babysitting wasn't far off the mark," he said to Eric, then joined his brother in sliding an arm around Emily's lower back and pulled her into his side, smirked at the deadbeat glaring back at him as he did. Yeah, he was just as possessive as Eric when it came to Emily Berringer and he didn't care who knew it.

She was theirs.

Matthew stared at them, obviously confused. "Babysitting?"

Eric chuckled. "Don't worry about it, kid. Private joke."

"Guys," Emily quietly scolded them.

"What the fuck is going on, Emily? Who the fuck are these guys?"

Emily looked up at him and then at Eric. "Um...."

"I'm Evan and he's Derek," Eric said, announcing the fake names they'd been given as part of their cover. "Who the fuck are you?"

Dane exchanged a quick look with his brother. They needed to get Emily out of there, but they also had a job to do and had to jump on opportunities as they presented themselves. And this little shit being Emily's date was an opportunity too good to pass up.

"I'm her boyfriend, arsehole."

Emily gasped, indignant. "You are *not* my boyfriend!" Then she looked up at Eric and added, "It's our first date."

So, the little jerk treated women the same way his older brother did. Like possessions. *Good to know.* Dane decided to push some buttons. They needed a way to meet this kid's brother and figured picking on him should do the trick. If anyone started hassling one of Dane's siblings, he'd want to knock the guy's block off, and he hoped this kid's brother felt the same way about him.

He laughed. "Your name is Arsehole? How much did your parents hate you?"

"You're the arsehole," the kid said through gritted teeth, then smirked as if he was about to drop some earth-shattering knowledge. "My name is Matthew. Matthew *Spencer*."

"Spencer, huh?" Eric said, his tone and demeanour unaffected by the news. "Any relation to Shane Spencer?"

The kid's smirk widened. "Yeah. He's my brother. And if you know who *he* is, then you should also know to be careful how you speak to me. Shane doesn't like it when people disrespect his family."

Dane snorted. "He won't much like us then." Then he leaned down and nuzzled Emily's earlobe. "Play along," he whispered, then kissed the side of her neck.

Emily's date continued glaring at them, drank down the rest of his beer, then tossed the bottle on the ground. If he'd hoped to intimidate them, he'd failed. Instead of smashing when it hit the bitumen, the bottle just bounced a bit then rolled away into the gutter. Matthew pouted at the thing as if it had betrayed him, then folded his arms across his chest. Another ridiculous attempt to look meaner than the petulant child he was.

Dane would have found the whole thing laughable if it wasn't for the simple fact that this kid's older brother was a sociopath. One who accrued power through fear and intimidation. He and Eric had zero time for people like that. People who used others, destroyed lives, and lost no sleep over it. Removing those people from society though, they had all the time in the world for that.

After a long moment of ineffectual scowling, Matthew held out his hand towards them, obviously expecting Emily to take it. When she didn't, he snatched at her and latched his hand around her wrist. "Let's go, Emily."

Crying out, she tried to yank her wrist free from his grip. "Let go of me."

"You came here with me."

"And she's going home with us."

In an instant, Eric had his hand around Matthew's throat, and not in the sensual way he'd done to Emily. His intention this time wasn't calm and controlled, it was violent. It was furious. "Take your hand off our woman."

The kid let her go and clawed at Eric's fingers. "Fuck you, man." The words were garbled as he struggled for air.

"Er—. Evan, let him go." Emily's voice shook as she reached up and laid her hand on Eric's shoulder, though he doubted it came from a place of concern for the kid. No. She'd never seen this side of Eric before. The possessive protector. "He's not worth it."

Eric's lip pulled back in a snarl, then he released the little shit with a shove, sending him stumbling backwards, away from Emily.

Rubbing at his throat, Matthew spat on the ground at their feet. "Take your slut and get out of here before my brother catches you disrespecting me."

Before either Dane or Eric could stop her, Emily stormed forwards and drilled a finger into the idiot's chest. "You call me a slut then talk about disrespecting *you*?" Her voice wasn't shaking now. She was downright pissed. And loud. "Well, fuck you, you little toad. You lied to me to get me to go out with you. You said you could hook me up, that I could get behind the wheel and race, but you had no intention of doing that, did you?" She pressed a hand to her chest, mockingly clutching at fake pearls. "A woman behind the wheel? God forbid!" And then she went straight back to glaring at the dumbstruck kid. "You chauvinistic mouth-breather."

Dane couldn't help the laughter that bubbled up from inside him. Watching Emily Berringer tear strips off Matthew Spencer was like watching a kitten tackle a pit bull. Probably dangerous, definitely ill-advised, but still, it was hands down the most entertaining thing he had seen in ages.

Until the little shit lifted his fist to strike her.

In an instant, both he and Eric moved to intervene, but not before Emily got in a shot of her own and slapped Matthew's cheek. The resounding *crack* of skin on skin was followed by a split second of silence, just enough time for her actions to register on her attacker's face, right before his expression contorted with rage.

Again he lifted his hand to hit her, but Emily blocked the blow and landed another hit of her own, turning his rage to shock. "Want another one?" she demanded, raising her fists and shifting her feet into a defensive stance.

Dane was impressed, though he shouldn't have been surprised. His sister, Karen—Emily's future sister-in-law— had been teaching Emily self-defence. A skill she herself had learned at an early age.

Obviously deciding against tempting fate one more time, Matthew returned to scowling at all of them. "You two need to control your bitch."

Eric folded his arms and chuckled. "Mate, the only bitch here is you."

Dane copied his brother. "Yeah, better luck next time, *Arsehole*."

The little shit glared at Emily for a long moment, then turned on his heel to leave, only to pull up short. "Where the fuck have you been?" he snapped.

"Move."

The one word command had him scuttling to the side, revealing the man of the hour. Shane Spencer. Known to the cops for a litany of reasons, but mostly illegal drag racing, intimidation, supplying party drugs to teens, and sexual assault. He was a very bad man, and he was staring at Emily like she was his next meal.

"Well hello there, cutie. And what's your name?"

Fuck.

Chapter Three

Emily immediately recoiled from the man standing in front of her. Unlike Matthew, who was about as intimidating as a paper straw, this guy oozed a vibe that screamed fuck around and find out.

And she did *not* want to find out.

Keeping an eye on the tattooed newcomer, she took a step back towards Eric and Dane before turning to face them, her shoulders slumped. The whole night had been a disaster. She'd been a complete idiot, had allowed her emotions to override her good sense more than once, and now she was just tired. "I wanna go home," she said, conceding defeat.

She never should have been there. Never should have agreed to go on a date with Matthew, the lying creep. She'd known he wasn't a particularly good guy—hell, the bloke had so many red flags he could stitch them into a Santa suit—but she'd been feeling abandoned and had greedily welcomed his attentions and the ego boost that had come with them. But she had also greatly overestimated her own abilities to play it cool in the face of danger.

Not to mention the fact she had potentially undone countless hours worth of work for Eric and Dane. Was that why they'd pulled back from her recently? Because they were working undercover? And she'd ruined everything with her foolishness.

Emily silently vowed then and there to make it up to them.

Somehow.

Eric held out his hand to her, his stern expression softening. "Let's go home."

"Not so fast."

Emily squeaked as she found herself being yanked backwards and pinned against the solid wall of malice behind her, one hand fisted in her hair, the other sliding across her stomach as he held her in place against his lean, muscled frame.

"Where do you think you're going, cutie?"

A second later, her eyes shot wide as Eric and Dane both whipped their arms up, guns held confidently in their outstretched hands and pointed at her captor's head. Where the hell had they been hiding those?

"Let her go!" Dane demanded, his expression one of barely contained rage. Eric, on the other hand, looked to be his usual calm and in control self, and if not for his clenched jaw and the muscle ticking in his cheek, she'd almost be fooled by the façade. She'd known these two men for a year, had talked, socialised and flirted with them relentlessly in that time and thought she knew them well enough to know their every mood.

She was wrong.

Emily had seen them happy, excited, mildly irritated, cheeky, horny, and protective, but she'd never seen this expression before. She'd never seen them look like they were ready—and willing—to kill another human being.

She'd done that. Her selfishness had put that look on their faces. On the one hand she was grateful to have two such amazing men looking out for her. On the other, she'd be lucky if they even gave her the time of day again after such a colossal fuck up.

And she didn't blame them one little bit.

"We don't want to kill you, Shane," Eric said. "But if you don't let go of our girl, we will."

The man behind her tsked at them as if they were naughty children, and she could almost hear the grin in his deep voice as he spoke, "Now, now, there's no need for that. We wouldn't want anyone to get hurt."

"Behind you!" Emily shouted, but it was too late. Two men appeared out of the crowd and pointed their own guns at Eric and Dane. "No!" She struggled against her captor, wincing against the pain in her scalp as her hair pulled taut. "Let me go, you sonofabitch! Leave them alone!"

"Oh, you're a feisty one. I like that." Then the scumbag leaned down and spoke softly, intimately in her ear, making her shudder. "But you're also a naughty girl, aren't you? Going on a date with my little brother when you're obviously with these two idiots?" He chuckled and slid his hand lower. Her stomach roiled. He raised his voice. "It's a good thing for you I like naughty girls more than I like my brother."

"Come on, man," his brother whined from somewhere behind them.

Keeping her gaze glued to Eric and Dane, she calmed her breathing and tried to focus. With guns trained on them, they were in no position to help her. She had to help herself. And when she felt Shane let go of her hair and slide his hand over her shoulder, she took her chance and used another move Karen had taught her in self-defence.

Latching both of her hands around Shane's wrist, Emily yanked his hand away from her belly and twisted to the side, ducked under his arm and heaved it upwards, forcing him to bend over, then kicked the back of his leg so he fell to his knees. Then she grabbed his thick fingers and yanked them backwards until he cried out.

"Leave them alone or I'll break your fingers," she snarled, the lingering pain in her scalp fuelling her temper. He grunted in pain but said nothing, so she began twisting his digits. "Do it. Now. Or you can try changing gears with a busted hand."

The arsehole craned his neck to look up at her, pure hatred written across his face, but his gaze still held a hint of lust. "You're so fucking hot." Her lip curled in disgust as he stared at her and licked his lips. "Do as she says," he barked at his cronies, and a moment later Eric was by her side, his weapon tucked safely away, and Dane pressed his gun to Shane's temple.

"You can let go now, kitten," Eric said, coaxing her into his arms.

"Give me a reason," Dane growled, but Eric shook his head.

"Leave it. Let's take her home."

A moment later, Dane had sheathed his weapon and joined his brother in herding Emily away from the danger. Heart pounding and hands shaking, she pressed her face into Eric's chest and breathed him in, the scent of him soothing her now that the adrenaline of the moment was wearing off. Had that really just happened? Had she actually threatened to break the fingers of a criminal?

"I can't believe that actually worked," she murmured,

her knees threatening to give out beneath her as they led her away.

Emily had threatened a criminal. That was a thing that had actually happened. Obviously she was suffering from temporary insanity. But she didn't want to think about it. She wanted to go home, take a long hot bath, and have a bloody good cry. But just when she thought the night couldn't get any worse, she heard Shane chuckle then raise his voice.

"Oh come on, don't run away," he said. They turned in time to see him levering to his feet and dusting himself off. "I thought you wanted to race. Isn't that why you agreed to go on a date with my shithead little brother?"

"Hey! I'm standing right here," Matthew said, gingerly probing at the bruise slowly taking shape on his cheek where she'd hit him.

His brother ignored him and grinned at Emily. "What do you say, cutie? Wanna race me?"

Eric's arm tightened around her, a warning to keep quiet and let him do the talking. "No," he said, the word landing with finality.

But Shane was undeterred. "I wasn't asking you."

A chorus of laughter and wooing erupted around them.

A challenge had been issued.

Emily looked up at Eric, then Dane. They were both glaring at Shane and the small crowd gathering around them, their brief yet violent interaction obviously of more interest than the hotted up Monaros and Mustangs they'd come out to see.

Inwardly, she cringed. She didn't know exactly what it was the Walker brothers were there to do, but she knew they were there to work, and knew she was screwing everything up for them. They were undercover for fuck's sake. The last thing they needed was an audience.

Or an idiot girl putting her foot in it at every given opportunity.

But... if there was even a slim chance she could put things right....

She turned her back to the crowd. "Would it help?" she said, keeping her voice quiet so only Eric and Dane would hear her.

"What?"

"If I raced him. Would it help?"

"No," Eric said at the same time Dane said, "Maybe."

Eric glared at his younger brother but Dane simply shrugged. "What? We wanted his attention. She got it. And you know she can drive."

"Her ability to drive was never in question—I *know* she can drive—but we're talking about Shane fucking Spencer." He slashed a hand through the air, cutting off the idea. "No."

Ignoring the happy fluttery feeling Eric's compliment caused around her heart, Emily straightened her spine and faced him down. "I can do this. You know I can."

"No. I won't allow it."

"Brother—" Dane began, coming to Emily's defence, but she cut him off.

"You won't allow it?" she repeated, her eyes narrowing and her knees feeling much more firm. "Huh. Last I checked, you can't tell me what to do, *Evan*. You're not my father."

Eric pulled her closer, pressed his lips to her ear, and the hard ridge of his cock against her hip. "Believe me, kitten, I am *very* aware of that fact. But that doesn't change the fact that you want to race a known psychopath who hates to lose, especially to women. And you've already humiliated him once tonight." He shook his head. "He will cheat. You will lose. I will *not* allow it."

"I'm waiting," Shane said behind them, managing to sound both irritated and bored at the same time.

Ignoring the twat behind them, Dane said quietly, "At this point, she may not have a choice."

"Would it help if I told you my brother was the one who taught me how to drive? You know, the one who outmanoeuvred professional car thieves? The one you insist on calling 'convict'?"

Eric's jaw tightened. "No, it wouldn't." Then he shook his head and blew out a slow breath, his irritation slowly morphing into resignation. "But Dane's right. We don't have a choice." He gripped her chin between his strong fingers but held her gently, and it took all of her will to focus on what he said next and not the zing of awareness between her thighs as he forced her gaze to his. God, she'd missed his touch. "You will drive Dane's car only, understand? If he insists on you driving one of his, we're getting you out of here. Agreed?"

Emily opened her mouth to argue, but the stern look on Eric's face made her think better of it. "Agreed," she mumbled, then turned to face her challenger and his groupies, folded her arms over her chest and lifted her chin. "What's in it for me?"

Shane smiled as if he knew he'd already won. It was disconcerting that such an evil man could have such a sexy smile. "I like a woman who knows what she wants."

"I highly doubt that," she replied, earning another round of childish wooing noises from the onlookers surrounding them. "And you didn't answer my question. What's it in for me if I race you?"

"I notice you didn't ask what you get if you win," Shane said, his entire demeanour relaxed and smug.

"Oh, I *know* I'm gunna win."

Shane snorted, then ran his tongue over his teeth and his smiled slipped into something more sinister. "All right. You win, you get my ride. But if I win...." His gaze trailed down her body and back up again, then he licked his lips. Sexy smile or not, her stomach churned and she knew exactly what was coming next. "You spend the night with me."

"No." Eric.

"Fuck no." Dane.

Emily smiled tightly at the unoriginal twat. "Doing what? Stroking your huge ego?"

"Oh, you'll be stroking something huge, cutie, and not just my ego."

Staring him down, Emily managed to control her urge to vomit, but only just. "Ew."

Chapter Four

The expression of shock on Shane Spencer's face as Emily dismissed his proposition using nothing more than mean girl energy would have been hilarious, if it hadn't immediately morphed into simmering fury with a side order of undisguised lust.

Eric watched their douchebag of a target run his gaze down Emily's curvy body again as he ran his tongue over his bottom lip, and the urge to shoot the arsehole had him itching to grab his gun. Not that he would lethally wound him or anything. No. He'd just maim him a little, or so he thought until Shane blew Emily a kiss.

Yeah. Okay. He'd maim him a lot.

"You got a car, cutie, or do you need a loaner?"

"Emily will drive my car," Dane said, a wicked grin crossing his brother's face as he proudly launched into the stats. "R8 GTS." He indicted the fierce red Holden parked a few metres away. "6.2 litre, upgraded cams, high flow injectors, and custom exhaust and headers. Plus cold air induction and a Superflow spoiler." His brother stared at Shane and held his gaze as he slid his hands over Emily's hips and pulled her back against him. Taunted him with what he'd never have. "She's sexy as fuck and when you drive her just right, she purrs like a wildcat in heat." He stared down at their girl. "The car's pretty damn near perfect too." Then Dane nuzzled against Emily's neck and made her squirm.

Eric grinned at the sight, at the blush colouring their girl's cheeks and the soft giggle escaping her kissable lips as Dane ravished her throat. *Fuck.* He was getting hard again. "Focus," he growled, the word aimed at all of them. They needed to stay sharp. Needed to keep Emily safe. He wouldn't be able to face her family if anything went wrong. And he didn't even want to contemplate what his sister would do to them if her newest BFF got hurt.

Dane pulled back and rested his chin on Emily's head, threw a smug grin at their target. "Your turn."

Shane folded his arms over his chest and lifted his chin. "Five litre Coyote Mustang GT." He nodded in the direction of the sleek black Ford surrounded by drooling idiots. "Upgraded injectors, headers and exhaust, custom rims, and twin turbos." His smile was almost demented. "My baby doesn't purr, she roars. You want perfection? She'll work your balls better than a hundred dollar hooker."

Emily snorted. "Then why the hell do you want to spend the night with me? Sounds like your *baby* will have you creaming your jeans before you even cross the finish line."

Eric burst out laughing, and so did a lot of their onlookers, including Shane's idiot brother.

Shane didn't like that. His eyes narrowed. "The first thing I'm gunna teach you, little girl, is some respect," he snarled at Emily.

"You can try," she threw back at him, the expression on

her face saying that was never going to happen. Not willingly, anyway. And it was Eric's job to make sure that scenario never came to pass. "But hey, if you guys have finished measuring your dipsticks, how about we get this race on the road?"

"All right!" Someone amongst Shane's groupies called out. "A V8 showdown."

"Ford versus Holden. Fuck yeah!"

"You got this, Shane! Smoke that bitch."

Cheers and whistles erupted from the gathered onlookers, then died just as fast when someone from the back of the crowd yelled out, "Cops! Go, go, go!"

The distant sound of sirens caught everyone's attention and the bulk of the spectators made tracks fast. Eric looked to Dane then Emily, who was still staring at Shane, still challenging him with nothing more than a tight smile and a raised eyebrow.

The arsehole's gaze tracked down her body one more time, then he blew her another kiss. "See you soon, cutie. You owe me a race." Then he too turned away and headed for his car.

Which also meant it was time to bail and take Emily home.

Eric grabbed her hand. "Let's get out of here."

"Really?" she said, and looked like she was about to say more before snapping her mouth shut and nodding. "Yeah. Okay."

Dane grabbed her other hand and they quickly found their way to their car and bundled Emily into the back seat. "Who the hell called them in?" his brother said, scowling as the engine roared to life.

"No idea," Eric said, watching Shane's black Mustang disappear into the traffic.

"Good Samaritan?"

"Lots of hotted up cars in a vacant carpark in Browns Plains on a Friday night? Yeah, I'm thinking good Samaritan. It's either that or we have a shadow," he said as they peeled out of the carpark.

"What are you two talking about? What's a shadow? And where are we going?"

Turning to look at Emily, Eric saw she wasn't buckled in. "Fasten your seatbelt," he scolded.

"What?" She glanced down at her lap. "Shit," she said, and quickly obeyed his command.

His brow furrowed as he studied her. It wasn't like her to forget something as simple or as important as fastening her seatbelt. "Look at me, kitten." She snapped her gaze to his, her obedience stirring his Dominant instincts, adding to his need to protect her. "Are you okay?"

She smiled and nodded. "Uh-huh."

But Eric knew Emily's smiles, and knew she was forcing it. His lips pinched together as he scowled at her. He'd have to keep a close eye on her, watch and make sure shock didn't take over and fill the void the adrenaline rush left in its wake.

She folded her hands in her lap and looked out the window. "You didn't answer my question. Where are you taking me?"

"Home," Dane replied.

"My home is in the opposite direction," she said, sighing softly as she leaned back in her seat, seemingly unbothered by the fact they weren't taking her directly home. Eric relaxed a little, knowing Emily still trusted them to take care of her, even after they'd essentially turned their backs on her for months.

He studied their girl for a moment longer before turning

to face the front. As much as she liked to think she was a capable young woman—and in many ways she absolutely was—she had no idea of the depth of the shit she'd just stood in.

"We're taking the long way 'round," Dane said, checking his mirrors. "We need to be sure we're not followed."

Shane Spencer had an inferiority streak a mile wide, and Emily had made a fool of him in public. The chances he was going to let that go were somewhere between Buckley's and none, which meant the chances of them being followed were high.

"Head for the motorway. If we have a tail, we can lose them in the Friday night traffic."

"I have done this before, you know?" Dane snapped.

His brother was irritated, and rightly so. Hell, Eric's emotions were also riding high after what they'd just been through, but he wouldn't let them get the better of him. He had to stay in control of himself, of the situation.

He had to keep them safe.

"We need to report this," he said.

"What about Emily? Can we keep her out of it?"

Eric shook his head. He'd love nothing more than to keep Emily well away from the fallout that was going to rain down on them after this, but knew they couldn't do that. They'd taken an oath to uphold the law, no matter what, even if it went against every protective instinct he had. "We have to do this by the book. We can't risk letting that arsehole get off on a technicality just because we wanted to keep Emily out of it."

Dane swore and hit the steering wheel with the heel of his palm. "You were right," he said. "Convict is going to kill us."

"No he won't," Emily said, the sharpness in her voice indicating her own heightened emotions. "And stop calling him that." Then she folded her arms over her chest and grumbled, "And stop talking about me like I'm not here. I hate it when people do that."

"We're sorry, kitten," Eric said, his jaw tightening as a throbbing ache started at the base of his skull. "We should have gotten you out of there sooner. You shouldn't be involved in any of this."

The gentle touch of Emily's hand on his shoulder made him jolt, then he turned to look at her again and watched her flick silent tears from her cheeks. "I'm sorry too," she said. "You're right. I shouldn't have been there. I never should have agreed to go out with Matthew. I just...." She sighed. "I was just...."

"What?" He needed to hear her say it. Needed to know how badly they'd screwed up by neglecting her for so long.

"Lonely."

Chapter Five

Emily said the word so softly, Dane almost didn't hear her over the sound of the traffic.

Lonely.

His brain almost imploded as his warring emotions collided. On the one hand, he was mad as fuck that he and Eric had made Emily sad, and on the other he wanted to whoop with joy knowing she'd missed them as much as they'd missed her.

The sooner they got this job done and went back to their normal lives the better.

Eric reached back and grabbed her hand. "We never meant for this to happen, kitten. We got pulled into this investigation at the last minute and we've been playing catch up ever since. The last two months have been insane." His brother scrubbed his free hand through his hair, his frustration bleeding out of him, making him look older than his thirty years of age. "Our lives are not our own right now, and I know that doesn't excuse what we did. We should have told you what was going on, but this is all new to us and—"

Emily leaned forwards between the seats. "No, it's okay. I mean, you did say you weren't going to be around much for a while, but I thought it was just an excuse. I thought...." She shook her head. "It doesn't matter what I thought. I get it now. You're undercover. You couldn't tell me." She sighed. "I imagine you couldn't tell anyone."

"Only our dad," Dane said.

As a retired cop himself, their father knew the challenges they faced on the job, especially when it came to balancing a life on the force with romantic relationships. Their own mother had walked out on them when they were just kids, saying she couldn't take it anymore, the not knowing if her husband was coming home each day. Wondering if she was going to be left alone with four kids to raise and no income besides a widow's pension.

At least that was the official version of events, the tale they were told as kids when their father was still blinded by his love for his wife. The truth was far more sordid.

Dane gritted his teeth and steeled his raging emotions. Now was not the time to be thinking about things like that. He had to focus. Had to make sure they weren't being followed, that he was doing his duty and keeping everyone safe.

Keeping Emily safe.

He checked his mirrors again, then changed lanes and exited the motorway, headed towards Eight Mile Plains. From there he could work his way north through the suburbs and into the heart of Brisbane, then backtrack to the safety of the Berringer estate. If they had a tail, there was no way they could hide themselves for that length of time.

They fell into a somewhat comfortable silence for the remainder of the trip, and a small smile tugged at his lips when they reached her parent's house in Sheldon, a rural residential area south of the city, and he saw Eric was still holding Emily's hand. Still seeking comfort in her touch.

"We're here."

Like many of the properties in the area, the Berringer estate was three acres of well concealed wealth. A dense border of trees and subtropical gardens hid a large two-storey house, a smaller guest house, a pool, and a full sized tennis court. But as they drove down the gently winding driveway, the true gem of the property—as far as Dane was concerned—came into view to the left of the main house.

A twenty car garage housing everything from a 1949 Healey Silverstone sports car to the 1968 Datsun Fairlady roadster his future brother-in-law had used to woo their sister. It was hoon heaven, and their two families had bonded quickly over their shared love of vintage metal and modern motorsports.

A separate, smaller garage housed their everyday vehicles closer to the house, and it was there that Dane parked his own car. He opened his mouth to speak but Eric held up a finger in a shhh motion, then nodded to the back seat. A quick look over his shoulder told him Emily had fallen asleep.

The way her long dark hair fell over her forehead and framed her pretty face entranced him. As did the gentle rise and fall of her chest as her soft snores escaped her. Emily was cute as fuck at the best of times, but watching her sleep eased something in Dane's chest he hadn't realised was tight. He could breathe easy again.

A smile tugged at one corner of his mouth. "Let's get her inside and put her to bed," he murmured, unbuckling his seatbelt as quietly as possible. Eric nodded and gently popped open his door.

Within moments, Dane had Emily scooped up in his arms, her face nestled in the crook of his neck, her arms wrapped tightly around his shoulders. Her warm, even breaths caressed his throat, and her long hair tickled his skin.

He'd missed this.

Missed the feel of her in his arms, the sound of her cute little moans when they kissed, or when he cupped her full breasts and murmured sweet dirty nothings in her ear.

Had it only been two months since they'd last touched her so intimately? It felt like a fucking eternity. And Emily was right, they might have spent months flirting hard, but they weren't dating. They had no right to be pissed off that she'd gone out with someone else, even if that someone was Matthew fucking Spencer.

Besides the flirting, some stolen kisses and a little light groping whenever they could manage to sneak away at barbeques, or bumped into each other somewhere around town, they hadn't even taken her on a proper date yet. They'd wanted to go slow and not scare her away with their unconventional brand of love. They'd wanted to build something more permanent with her. Something real. And then they'd had their lives turned upside down and everything had gone to shit.

But Emily *was* theirs.

Dane had felt it down to his bones from the moment they'd met her a year ago. She had invaded his every waking thought ever since. Most of his dreaming thoughts too.

And he knew Eric felt the same.

He also knew their situation wasn't considered normal. Two brothers loving the one woman? Without jealousy or coming to blows? It was unheard of, right?

Wrong.

Dane and his older brother had always been this way. As soon as they'd figured out what love was they'd known their kind of love was different. Eric wasn't just his big brother, he was his best friend, and Dane knew they could make Emily happy.

Together.

When they reached the front door, Eric gingerly searched Emily's pockets for her keys, trying carefully not to wake her.

"If you wanted to feel me up, you only had to ask." Her amused voice was muffled against his neck.

Dane chuckled even as Eric scowled. "Have you been awake this whole time?" his brother scolded.

Emily lifted her head and smiled sheepishly. "Only since you pulled me out of the car," she said.

"You want me to put you down?" Dane asked, returning her smile.

"Don't you dare," she said, and snuggled even tighter against him.

Eric huffed a laugh and shook his head. His brother couldn't stay mad at her anymore than he could. "Kitten, where's your door key?"

"Front left pocket."

Dane juggled Emily in his arms to give Eric access to her jeans pocket and a moment later his brother had the door open and ushered them both inside the house.

"I'll do a perimeter check," he said quietly. "You do a sweep of the house."

Putting her back on her feet, Dane pressed a quick kiss to Emily's lips, then whispered, "Stay here." He waited until she nodded, then palmed his weapon and did as Eric had asked, clearing the house, room by room.

When he returned, he found Emily in the kitchen,

making a sandwich. He scowled at her as he put his gun away. "I thought I told you to stay put out there," he said, pointing to the foyer.

She half shrugged then took a bite of her sandwich. "I got hungry," she said around the mouthful of food.

Just as Dane opened his mouth to chastise her, Eric strode into the kitchen. They nodded to each other. There were no signs of the Spencer brothers or their goons. They were safe.

Eric started making a sandwich of his own. "When are your parents due home?"

"A couple of weeks," Emily said. "They left London yesterday, so they'll be in Paris now. They're staying there for a week for their anniversary, then driving down to Madrid for a few days, then flying over to Florence, driving to Rome, doing all of the touristy things there, then flying home."

"And Easton?"

Emily rolled her eyes at the mention of her younger brother then smiled tightly. "Enjoying his gap year and visiting our grandparents in Western Australia." Her smile disappeared. "He won't be home until the end of the month."

"So you're home alone then?"

Her brows pulled together as she finished her sandwich, then she dusted her hands off and folded her arms over her delectable chest. "What's with the interrogation? Are all of these questions leading somewhere...,"--her expression softened, turned cheeky,--"the bedroom perhaps?" She stepped into Dane's personal space, slid her hands over his chest and grinned up at him. "Now that you know we're all alone and not likely to be interrupted."

He wanted to return her grin but couldn't. Not yet. He

grabbed her wrists, removed the distraction that was her seductive touch and held her firm. "Does Matthew know where you live?"

Dane hated to ask the question but he had to be sure. Just because the Spencer brothers weren't waiting for them when they got home, didn't mean they wouldn't show up at some point in the near future. And there would be no sexy fun times until he was certain she was safe.

Her grin faltered. "What? No."

"Are you sure?" Eric asked.

"Pretty sure." She didn't sound sure.

"He picked you up tonight, correct?" She nodded. "Where from?"

"I met him outside of work. I left my car there, at the dealership. Why?" She looked from him to Eric. "You don't think he'd actually come looking for me, do you?"

A muscle ticked in Eric's jaw. "I don't know. I'm more concerned about what his brother will do. He's the one who worries me."

"You were right," Dane said. "We have to report this. Especially if there was a shadow. We have to get in front of this."

"What's a shadow? What are you talking about?"

Eric sighed and scrubbed a hand through his messy hair. "A shadow is another undercover cop attached to the investigation. They're usually a senior officer, someone more experienced in undercover work who shadows newbies and can step in if shit goes sideways."

"Like an idiot girl trying to race a psychopath?" Emily said, her shoulders slumping as she stared at the floor, her remorse as plain as day. "That kind of shit?"

Dane cupped her chin in his hand, lifted her gaze to

meet his. "You weren't to know what you were stepping into."

"But I knew Matthew wasn't a good guy, and I went with him anyway." She tilted her head back and groaned. "I'm so stupid! And now you have to clean up *my* mess. That's the thing you need to get in front of, right? The trouble I caused you both tonight."

There was no point hiding the truth from her. Dane nodded. "Yes."

Chapter Six

Emily pushed the heels of her palms against her eyes and growled at her own ineptitude. Why had she thought it would be a good idea to go against the grain and do something she wouldn't usually do? When had that ever worked out in her favour?

Never, that's when.

Every time she'd even thought about doing something out of character, she got screwed. And not in a fun way.

To add insult to injury, her fuck up was now causing Dane to keep her at a distance instead of pulling her close like he would have done before tonight, and Eric hadn't stopped scowling at her.

Because she hadn't just fucked up.

Nope. She'd fucked everything *alllll* the way up. Not just for herself, but for people she cared about deeply.

As much as she tried to hold them in check, hot tears began spilling down her cheeks and this time they did not stay quiet. "I'm so sorry," she sobbed. "I never meant to cause anyone any trouble, but I get it now. I get why my brother did what he did all those years ago." She shook her head, chastised herself for not seeing what had been right in front of her face for so long. "I never understood why Teddy and Dad were always butting heads but I get it now. I *totally* get it."

In an instant she was surrounded, enveloped by masculine heat and strength as Dane pulled her into his arms and pressed her head to his chest, and Eric rubbed his hands against her back and stroked her hair. She'd been sandwiched between them like that before, but always in a sexual way. Their touch had always been exciting to her, arousing. Now they stroked their hands down her arms and over her hips, pressed kisses to her face and hair, but none of it was sexual. Instead, she felt safe. She felt cared for.

Loved.

And it made her cry even harder. She'd been holding her emotions in check for so many years, she'd begun to think she'd never let them out, but now that she knew she was free to let her feelings loose, her misery refused to be shoved down any longer.

"I've been so alone," she sobbed, her words muffled against Dane's shirt. "All I do is work and study, then work some more. I don't have any friends. I don't go out. I don't even have time to read smutty romance books anymore. And as for a gap year?" She scoffed and angrily swiped at her tears. "I never got a fucking gap year. I have no life outside of the dealership." She sniffed and wiped at her nose. "That place has owned my arse since I finished high school." Her tears welled up again. "And I don't even like BMWs."

Suddenly, she felt their bodies begin to shake, heard their soft snorting as they tried to contain their laughter, and she stiffened in their arms. But the longer she stood there, the more she realised they weren't laughing at *her* exactly, just her bratty behaviour.

Most people should be so lucky to have her level of privilege and yet there she was, acting like an entitled twat in front of two of the most hardworking men she'd ever known. Men who worked everyday with people doing it tough, who had themselves grown up on the other side of the tracks, and probably understood privilege better than most. Especially when people abused it. Or used it to justify abusing others.

Suddenly the pity party dancing around in circles in her head came to a screeching halt and she huffed out an awkward laugh. "I'm such an idiot."

"Yeah," Dane agreed, nodding as he grinned down at her. "But you're our idiot."

"I really am sorry. For everything."

"We know, kitten," Eric said. "We're sorry too."

Emily nibbled at her lip before looking up at them again. "You could have told me you know? Not all the nitty-gritty details, obviously, but you could have said *something*. Let me know *why* you weren't going to be around as much. I would have understood if you'd told me it was a work thing," she said. "I would have waited."

Dane pulled her into his arms again and squeezed her to him. "We wanted to, baby. But we were under strict orders not to say anything." He sighed. "We only had permission to tell one person so we told Dad."

"We never wanted to leave you alone," Eric said. "We only wanted to keep you safe."

"I know that now." Emily wiped her eyes with the back of her hand, then looked up at the brothers from beneath her lashes. "But you acted so distant. I thought you'd changed your minds about me, that you'd had your fun and didn't want me anymore. Then Matthew started coming around the dealership and he made it *very* clear he wanted me. I was flattered by his attention, and he didn't seem—I don't know—intimidated, I guess, that I knew so much about cars. A lot of guys hate that, but he didn't. So when he asked me out, I didn't really think about it. I just said yes, because...." She half shrugged and looked away.

Eric slid his knuckles along the line of her jaw, hooked one under her chin and forced her to look at him. "You were lonely."

Tears leaked down her cheeks again, but Eric leaned in and kissed them away. When he pulled back to stare at her, his eyes had darkened, the blue turned stormy. Sliding his hand from her chin to her throat, he stroked his thumb against her pulse. "You need to rest, kitten."

Emily leaned into his touch, a rising sense of pleasure overshadowing her sadness. "You're not making me feel very restful."

Moving to stand beside his brother, Dane chuckled and grinned at her. "What is he making you feel, baby?"

Her tongue flicked out and moistened her lips as she stared at Dane's mouth, willing him to kiss her again. "Horny."

"That's our girl," he said, then stole her away from Eric and granted her wish, kissing her thoroughly, deeply, lashing his tongue against hers. Making love to her with his mouth.

"I have to make a call," Eric said, then fisted his hand in Emily's hair and yanked her away from Dane, stole her kiss for himself. Stole the very air from her lungs and left her breathless. "But when I get back," he growled against her lips, "we're going to teach you a lesson you won't readily forget."

Her whole body shivered with anticipation. "Oh?"

Wrapping his other hand around her throat again, he held her still, made sure she couldn't look away from his intense blue stare. "You need a reminder." He bared his teeth. "You're ours. *Only* ours." Then he let her go and took a step back, as if he was afraid of what he would do next if he stayed too close to her, but he held her gaze for what felt like an age. "Take her upstairs and get her ready for bed," he said to Dane. "I'll join you as soon as I can." Then he turned and left the kitchen and she couldn't stop the compulsion to watch him walk away, her gaze glued to his spectacular arse.

The man filled out a pair of jeans better than anyone else she knew. Almost anyone else.

"Tell me truthfully," Dane murmured close to her ear, his own strong denim clad legs bracing against hers as they watched Eric through the glass sliding doors. The hard length of his cock nestled against her arse. "How wet is your pussy right now?"

Emily pressed her thighs together and pushed her arse out, rubbed against Dane's cock. His crass way of speaking never failed to turn her on, especially when it was layered on top of Eric's dominance. "Why don't you take me upstairs and find out?"

"I would love nothing more than to sink into your sweet cunt, baby," Dane said, turning her to face him, "but there will be no sex tonight."

"Why not?" She pouted.

He smoothed her hair away from her face, the heat from his hands sinking into her skin, warming her in more ways than one. "Because it's been a big night for all of us," he said, his tone sinking into something more serious, "and I don't think it has hit you yet exactly how close you came to getting hurt tonight."

Emily pursed her lips, then shook her head, as if trying to dislodge the memory of Shane's hands on her body. "I know I screwed up, but everything is fine now."

Dane's mouth pulled into a tight line and his brow furrowed. "Everything is definitely *not* fine."

Her need to be closer to him had her fisting her hands in his shirtfront. "I've already apologised for messing up your work tonight," she said quietly.

Dane's shift in mood was making her nervous. She'd never seen him like this, heard him like this. As if he was disappointed in her.

"This has nothing to do with our work and everything to do with you, Emily." He grabbed her hand and started towards the stairs, practically dragging her behind him. He wasn't disappointed, he was mad. "This wall you hide behind, it's not going to work with us." He stopped at the top of the stairs and stared down at her, his frown deepening. The expression didn't sit as well on his face as it did on Eric's. "You don't need to hide your feelings from us, baby."

Her mouth fell open as her brain scrambled for a retort but the best she could come up with was, "What wall? I'm not hiding anything."

"You've been hiding a lot of things from us," Dane said, then dragged her the rest of the way to her bedroom and stood her at the foot of her bed. "But that all ends tonight."

Emily couldn't help poking the bear. This was Dane after all, not Eric. He was horny, not a hard arse... usually. "Oh? And what are you going to do about it?"

His response was to grin and lift his chin in the direction of the doorway. She turned and found Eric standing there, watching her with his signature scowl and stormy gaze, and a sudden knot of emotions formed in her throat, cutting off any further smartarsery.

Backing away from the dominant devil, she was quickly caught again by Dane, his strong arm banding around her waist as he held her captive against his chest. His warm breath brushed the shell of her ear. "Careful what you wish for, baby."

Chaos reigned inside her, her heart suddenly beating so fast it couldn't possibly be good for her, and her emotions went to war with one another. As Eric slowly closed the distance between them, his dark gaze locked on hers, her lust and need were engaged in a battle for dominance with her uncertainty and dread, and by the time he stopped in front of her, Emily wasn't sure which camp had won the war, just that her skin felt ready to combust and her panties were soaked.

And then he dropped his hands to his belt buckle. "Strip her."

Chapter Seven

"But... Dane said we weren't going to have sex."

Eric bit back a smile even as his ego preened. He was sure Emily had meant for her words to sound accusatory more than disappointed, but she hadn't quite nailed it. And he was man enough to admit he liked the thought she was upset they wouldn't be fucking her tonight. Truth be told, he was pretty pissed off about the whole situation too. He and Dane finally had their girl alone and at their mercy, and they were going to waste the opportunity by punishing her.

But it had to be done.

She had to learn, to know that what she'd done was unacceptable.

She had knowingly put herself in a dangerous situation and it could not—would not—happen again.

"Dane was right. There will be no sex tonight. We don't reward bad behaviour."

"Arms up," Dane said, proceeding with Eric's instructions to undress their woman. Emily folded her arms across her chest instead. *So stubborn.*

"What bad behaviour?" she demanded, scowling up at him. "I know I screwed up your undercover job but I've already apologised for that. Repeatedly. What else can I do?"

"What can you do? You can listen when we tell you this has nothing to do with our job and everything to do with you putting yourself in danger. What you can do is take your punishment like a good girl."

"Punishment?" Emily visibly swallowed as she wriggled against Dane's chest, but his brother's grip was much stronger than her attempt to escape him. She moistened her lips, the action drawing Eric's attention, then launched into her defence. "I know, okay? I shouldn't have gone out with Matthew. I saw the red flags and I ignored them, but I honestly didn't think he would take me to an illegal drag race, or that people would be selling drugs right out in the open. I mean, who does that, right? But I had my phone, and I was just about to call Teddy to come and pick me up when I saw Dane and I felt—" She dropped her gaze and stared at the floor.

"What did you feel when you saw me, baby?"

Eric slid a knuckle under her chin and lifted her face, but she refused to meet his gaze. "Look at me, kitten," he said, keeping his voice soft. She had to learn to stop hiding from them, and that might be easier if he wasn't his usual grumpy self. He hated the silent tears that tracked down her cheeks, how she nervously shifted her weight from one foot to the other. Leaning down, he kissed away her tears. "Talk to us, Emily," he said. "What did you feel when you saw Dane?"

She rolled her bottom lip between her teeth and bit down, as if she was trying to keep her words inside, but one slipped out. "Safe," she whispered, finally looking up at him again. "I felt safe, because I knew if Dane was there, you wouldn't be far away. I felt safe knowing both of you were there, knowing you'd take care of me."

"Even though we haven't been around much lately?" Dane pushed. "Even though you thought we'd lost interest in you?"

Her tears fell faster, thicker, and she sniffed loudly. "Yes."

"Why?" Eric asked. "Why would you trust us after we abandoned you?"

It hurt to say those words. They hadn't abandoned her, but she hadn't known that at the time, and what she said next would determine how many lashes of his belt she got, if she got any at all. They needed to teach her a lesson in safety, something she wouldn't forget, but at that moment all Eric really wanted to do was pull her into his arms and hold her tight, tell her she was theirs, that they were hers, that this whole thing had just been a colossal fuck up.

But there was another reason to punish her. Another lesson to be taught. One that was long overdue.

"Because you're cops," she said quietly, and dropped her gaze again. "I knew you'd do the right thing."

Eric looked at his brother and thanked God Emily couldn't see his expression. Dane already hated this under-cover gig they'd had thrust upon them, but now he looked like he wanted to burn the world to the ground.

Emily knew they'd do the right thing. Not because she knew them intimately, not because they loved her or—hopefully—because she loved them. No. She knew they would keep her safe because they were cops. Because it was their fucking job, the thing they were *paid* to do.

Despair gut-punched him so hard he thought he might vomit.

She'd given up on them.

Completely.

Eric shook his head, rejected the idea. No. Fuck that. Emily wasn't giving up. They wouldn't let her, and before he could even think about what he was doing, his hand latched around Emily's throat and squeezed just enough make sure he had her full attention. Her eyes grew wide, her pupils dilated, and her plump lips parted on a gasp.

"Did you try contacting us at all in the last two months?" he said. "Even once?"

She tried to shake her head. "No."

"You saw Kiki every week for one reason or another," Dane added. "Did you ask her where we'd gone or what we were doing?"

Her eyes narrowed. "You said you didn't tell Karen what you were up to."

"We didn't. But do you really think she wouldn't have kicked our butts to get you answers if you'd wanted them?" Eric felt her hammering pulse against his fingers, saw the myriad of emotions dancing in her pretty eyes. Saw the storm she didn't know how to navigate. But that's why she had them. They would be her compass, her anchor, her safe harbour. They would take care of her. But first they had to tear down the walls she was constantly rebuilding against them. "Why did you give up on us so easily?"

"Easy?" Her lip curled and then the storm exploded. "You think losing you was easy?"

"You didn't lose us, baby," Dane said, tightening his grip as she struggled to free herself from his arms.

"How was I supposed to know that? You were there one minute and gone the next!"

"Why didn't you reach out to us, Emily? Not one call.

Not one text. By your own admission, you didn't even ask our sister about us. Why?"

"Because you abandoned me," she yelled, stamping her foot against the carpet and narrowly missing Dane's foot. "You ghosted me. And I learned a long time ago not to bother chasing after men who obviously had no interest in being with me. Why wouldn't I think you were done with me? I'm short, overweight, and boring. Not to mention—"

"Not to mention what?" Eric said, his fingers flexing around her throat in warning.

A warning she ignored completely as she continued disparaging herself. She scoffed. "Well, I'm not exactly winning any beauty contests over here, am I?" Angry tears fell thick and fast as she glared at him. "I always knew my time with you two would end, I knew I was nothing more than a temporary distraction...." She cast her gaze to the side, away from him again. "Or worse."

"What could possibly be worse than you thinking we don't want you?" Dane growled, tightening his grip again as Emily tried to shove away from him.

"Using me."

Dane stared at the back of Emily's head, confusion writ across his face. "For what?"

"As a way of getting back at my brother for dating your sister. I hear how you speak to him, the disdain you have for him."

Eric's head lolled back until he was staring at the ceiling, then he let loose a long sigh. This fucking undercover bullshit was ruining their lives. And the urge to hold Emily tight suddenly overwhelmed every other sense he had, but he had to wait. Just a little longer.

Straightening up, he dropped his hand from her throat. "Let her go."

Dane's gaze snapped to his, and panic sat heavy in his voice. "Eric, what are you doing?"

"Getting a few things straight," he said, and folded his arms over his chest. "First, we have nothing but respect for your brother. What Teddy did all those years ago, what he sacrificed to keep you and your family safe, that took guts. And do you really think we would let him anywhere near our sister if he hadn't already proven himself to be a good man?"

"He takes care of her," Dane added, mirroring Eric's stance. "He makes her happy, and if you think he doesn't give as good as he gets when we tease him, then you haven't been paying attention."

Eric moved closer until the toes of his boots bumped into the tips of Emily's sneakers. It forced her to look up at him and stumble slightly, but he caught her upper arms and held her steady. She gasped at his touch, at his nearness, and he welcomed the sweet sound. Couldn't wait to make her gasp for other, more pleasurable reasons.

"Second, you were *never* temporary, kitten." He brushed her hair away from her face. "And you certainly weren't some kind of payback against your brother."

"Yeah, right."

"It's true, baby. We've wanted you from the moment we saw you."

"We're not conventional men, Emily. We don't love the way regular people do. And we know from past experience that it takes a certain type of woman to appreciate that about us. That's why we took our time getting to know you, why we didn't rush. We wanted—*want*—something real with you. But maybe we took too long. Maybe we should have told you months ago how we feel about you. Maybe it is our fault that you gave up on us. But maybe—just maybe

—if I tell you now how head over heels in love with you we are, maybe you'll forgive us."

"What did you say?" Her confusion was adorable.

Eric smiled and stroked his knuckles along her jaw and over her cheek, revelled in the warmth and softness of her skin. "I said I love you, kitten."

Dane rested his hands on her shoulders, let her know he had her back, always, then kissed the side of her neck. "And I love you too, baby."

She started to shake her head, rejecting what they were saying to her, so Eric caught her chin in his hand and held her firm. "You don't have to say it back if you're not ready. We realise it's a lot, that we're a lot. Just tell us you believe us. Say you'll be ours. That you belong to us."

"Both of us."

"Because we are yours, Emily. If you still want us."

Emily sniffed and wiped her cheeks dry then stared blankly, as if they had just said the most ludicrous thing imaginable. "You... love me?"

Chapter Eight

"Baby, look at me."

Turning her to face him, Dane cupped Emily's cheeks in his hands and stared deeply into her bewildered gaze. He understood her confusion, her mistrust of what they were saying to her, but the level of disbelief in her voice broke his heart.

They'd already agreed they wouldn't have sex with her yet, their emotions were too heightened. Hell, Eric had to stop him from putting a fucking bullet in Shane Spencer's brain, and all because that scumbag had dared to put his hands on their girl and whispered foul things in her ear.

It didn't get much more heightened than that, and he certainly didn't want his first time with Emily being marred by the anger still swirling around in his head.

And yet, as he stared into Emily's eyes and watched her overactive imagination pinball back and forth as she tried to decipher their declaration of love, he felt a sense of calm wash over him, through him. Diminish that anger a little more.

She was there, with them.

Like she always should have been.

"I get it, baby. I do. You've had so much shit thrown at you tonight, and we're just piling it on even more. It's overwhelming, isn't it? Your body is telling you one thing, your brain is telling you something different, but in your heart you know what's right. You know Eric and I mean what we say. That we love you." He shook his head. "We don't expect you to say it back. Not yet, but—"

"Shut up." Emily pressed her fingertips to Dane's mouth, and her eyes cleared and focussed on him with pinpoint accuracy. "My brain is telling me to run away and hide, that it's all too much, that I can't trust you."

"Kitten," Eric murmured, his gaze glued to Emily and his hands fisted by his sides, but she held her hand up to him too, silencing whatever he was going to say.

"But... my body is screaming out for you to touch me, to hold me, to prove me wrong and make me stay. And my heart?" She shook her head. "My heart feels too big in my chest, as if it might explode if I don't tell you right now how much I love you too. How much I love both of you," she said, reaching for Eric.

His brother moved and stood beside him as they smiled down at Emily. And while he didn't know exactly what Eric felt, if it was anything like the relief coursing through him, Dane could imagine well enough.

Emily loved them. She was theirs.

Finally.

"Hold me," she whispered, her gaze darting between the pair of them. "Please. I've missed you both so much."

In an instant, she was wedged between them. Eric at her front, her shield. Dane at her back, her protector. They held her as she quietly sobbed, as her body shook. They held her until she sagged between them, until she lifted her tear-stained face and smiled up at them, a mixture of love and contentment and renewed confidence blanketing her expression as she sniffed loudly and wiped away her tears.

"So what happens now?" she asked.

Eric leaned down and kissed her, a brief peck on her sweet mouth. "Now you let Dane undress you."

"Okay," she sighed, reaching back to wrap her arms around Dane's neck.

Taking advantage of her position, he slid his hands over her breasts and gently squeezed them. Emily settled against him even more, so he nuzzled against her neck, nibbled and licked his way to her earlobe, then bit down. Her little moans of pleasure coupled with the way her luscious arse rubbed against his jeans sent a jolt of lust directly to his dick, but he also knew Eric hadn't finished speaking, and knew Emily wasn't going to like what would happen next.

Sliding one hand down to her waist, he deftly unfastened her jeans and slid his hand inside, then flicked his gaze to Eric and nodded.

His brother's gaze darkened, his voice roughened, his dominant side taking over. "Now you take your punishment like a good girl."

"What? No! Why?"

Before Emily could put up a fight, Dane slid a finger deep inside her pussy. She was so tight, so fucking wet, he easily slid in another. She squirmed against him, her moan almost a whimper as he softly stroked her.

"I thought we'd settled this," she whined, then moaned, her head lolling against his shoulder.

"We haven't settled anything yet," Eric said, his usual stern expression back in place. "Not completely."

"But." She panted. "Oh, God...." She thrust her hips against Dane's hand, tried to push her clit against the heel of his palm. Tried to control the situation. Like he'd let that happen.

Dane removed his fingers and grinned at her frustrated whimper and the way she stamped her foot again. "Bad girl," he growled in her ear.

"But," she tried again, wriggling her arse against his cock, "you told me you love me, and I told you I love you, and now you want to beat me? And I still don't understand why. You said I didn't mess up your work."

"He's not going to beat you, Emily," Dane said, tightening his grip on her breast. "A beating means maliciously inflicting harm. He would never do that to you."

Eric stroked his fingers across her forehead and brushed a stray lock of hair off her face. "But I am going to discipline you. You've earned that much at the very least. And as to the why, well,"—he grinned—"where to begin?"

"I—" Her mouth flapped open and closed as she stared at his brother, then she turned her ire on Dane, attempted to glare at him over her shoulder.. "And what about you? Are you just going to stand there and watch him do this to me?"

"Of course not," Dane said, his tone offended. "I'm going to help him."

Emily's outraged gasp quickly morphed into another moan as he slid his fingers deep inside her again. "This is so unfair," she whined, panting her words into being as Dane stroked in and out of her. "You can't use my horniness against me."

Dane chuckled and circled his thumb around her swollen clit, making her gyrate against him. "Apparently I can."

"Arms up, kitten. Show me what a good girl you can be."

Finally realising she had no option but to obey, she

made the cutest little growling sound before doing as Eric commanded and lifted her arms above her head.

"Good girl," Dane whispered in her ear.

He quickly had her T-shirt off, followed by her shoes, jeans and underwear, then he took a step back and joined his brother. "Beautiful," they said in unison, their eyes raking over every stunning inch of her curvy body.

Emily stood before them, completely naked, a pink blush decorating her cheeks even as she tried to glare at them, with one foot tapping against the carpeted floor and her hands anchored to her hips. Not exactly the picture of a demure, submissive woman.

But then again, she never had been.

That was one of the things they loved most about her. Her fighting spirit, her fearlessness.

Although after tonight, reckless might be a more appropriate description.

"Hands by your side, Emily," Eric said, cocking one brow when she took a little too long to obey. "Stand still."

Emily opened her mouth to respond but Dane pressed a finger to his lips in a shush motion, sighing contentedly when she did as instructed. He wasn't as dominant as Eric, never had been, never would be, but he did enjoy the trust she put in him, in them. She knew they would never hurt her. Not intentionally anyway.

She wouldn't be so quick to obey them if she didn't.

Their only wish was to keep her safe and happy. To let her know they had her back no matter what. To show her how deeply they cared for her so the shitshow that happened that night would never happen again.

With all of her naked splendour on display, the anticipation was driving Dane crazy.

He ached in a way he never had before. It was more

than physical, more than the hard-on aching to be released from his jeans. His heart had hurt to see her tonight, to know the danger she was in simply by being there. Christ only knew what Shane and his cronies would have done to her had they found out he and Eric were cops.

The fact remained that Emily might still be in danger.

He wasn't sure what had been said during Eric's earlier phone call back to base, but the expression on his brother's face as he'd entered the room wasn't encouraging.

"Have you figured it out yet, kitten?" Eric continued, pulling his belt free from the loops on his jeans. "Do you know why I'm going to punish you tonight?"

Her mouth pressed into a mulish line, Emily continued to glare at them. "Because I went on a date with someone else?" she guessed, and lifted one shoulder in a shrug.

Eric folded his belt in half, making sure the buckle was secured in his palm, then shook his head as though he were disappointed in her answer. "No. I'm punishing you because you gave up on us, and *then* you went out with someone else."

Emily's hands fisted by her sides, but when she opened her mouth to respond no words came out, just the sound of frustrated irritation.

"You knowingly put yourself in danger—don't deny it— and for that alone you deserve a bloody good whipping," Eric said, tapping his belt against the side of his leg. "But you committed one other sin tonight, one you're guilty of committing before. One we should have put a stop to well before now."

Finding her voice again, Emily said, "Oh? And what's that?"

"No one—*no one*—calls our girl names," Dane said. "Especially not our girl."

Chapter Nine

"What names?" Emily's frustration turned to confusion in the blink of an eye.

"Short, fat, boring," Dane counted off his fingers as he listed the insults Emily had levelled at herself.

"I never said fat."

"It was strongly implied," Eric said, frowning at her. "Do you really think so little of yourself? So little of us? Do you honestly think we would toy with you like that? That we lied when we told you how much we adore you."

"Did you think we faked our hard-ons when we touched you?" Dane added, and grabbed the front of his jeans, showing off another obvious erection.

"Or that we took advantage of you when we stole your kisses?" Eric added.

"We love every luscious curve of your body, baby. Every soft inch."

"And we have missed your softness, your warmth." Eric's gaze bored into hers. "We've missed your kisses and your eagerness for our touch."

Dane lifted his fingers to his nose and inhaled, the fingers he'd had deep inside her. "And we've missed your sweet scent." His tongue flicked out and wrapped around his fingers and his eyelids fluttered closed. "Missed your intoxicating taste."

Feeling her cheeks heat again, Emily ducked her head in an attempt to hide her reaction from them. The last thing she needed was to add fuel to their fire. "You're not supposed to be enjoying this," she grumbled.

"On the contrary," Dane said. "*You're* not supposed to be enjoying this. We're going to enjoy every fucking second of it."

Eric stepped in front of her, hooked a knuckle under her chin and lifted her face to his. His usual stoic expression greeted her, but even she couldn't miss the warmth in his eyes as he stared down at her, or the concern in his deep voice when he spoke. "We've left you alone for too long, kitten, let you get in your own head for too long." He stroked his fingertips along the edge of her jaw, the gentleness of his touch making her shiver with need. "You've been lying to yourself and you don't even know it. But that stops here and now."

"It does?" Even Emily couldn't miss the hint of hope in her voice.

"Do you trust us?" Eric asked.

Staring into his eyes, she saw the determination and the quiet strength that always radiated from him. Then she looked to Dane and his smiling face, and saw the warmth and adoration he had never concealed from her.

Her insides shook with a jumble of emotions until she couldn't tell one apart from another. Hope, desperation, loneliness, love.

None of it made sense.

Emily had always projected the aura of a strong and capable woman, but in reality her confidence was a façade, one that was easily dented. But the longer she stood there, debating her answer to Eric's question, the more she realised... they already knew this about her. Had probably always known. And here she'd always thought herself clever enough to hide it from them. Apparently she was wrong.

Her men had known all along that she was a fraud... and they loved her anyway.

And she loved them. She had for ages. That's why it had hurt so much when they had just disappeared, why she'd written them off so quickly. Better that than succumb to her heartache and let everyone see how weak she truly was.

As much as it sucked to admit, if there was a way to get past it, a way to push through all the resentment she had built up around herself, she knew this was it.

She would take her punishment.

She would cry and scream and curse blue bloody murder if it meant they could go back to the way they were before, when they stole kisses and whispered sweet words and made her feel like the luckiest woman in the world.

"Yes. I trust you."

"Then let us take care of you, kitten," Eric said. "Not because you think it's our job to do so, but because you are important to us." He slid his hand around her throat and held her steady, would not let her look away from him. "Do you understand?"

"Yes."

Eric's hand flexed around her neck. "Yes, *Sir*," he said, his voice taking on a sharper tone.

Emily's thighs involuntarily clenched together as a jolt of sensation lit up her clit. She moistened her lips and tried to duck her head, to give herself a moment to compose herself, but Eric wouldn't let her. Her throat rolled against his palm as she swallowed and tried again. "Yes, Sir," she said, her voice little more than a breathy whisper.

Eric's mouth softened and one corner lifted in the slightest of smiles. "Good girl."

And there was that sensation again, making her thighs come together in an attempt to stem the electric zing that was somehow focussing all of her attention on her pussy. She'd felt it before, to a lesser extent, when Dane had caught her alone amongst the shelves in Novelteas book-shop and whispered dirty nothings in her ear before licking her throat and kissing her breathless. And when Eric had followed her into the walk-in-pantry at their last family barbeque, where he'd slipped his hand inside her bra and pinched her nipples between his rough fingertips.

But those zings had been minor blips on her radar. This sensation was stronger, more compelling, made her want to do... *things.*

Things she probably should be ashamed of, would have been ashamed of if she'd been with anyone other than Eric and Dane.

Releasing her throat, Eric moved to the bed and sat on the edge of it, placed his belt beside him, then grinned and patted his knee. "Lie across my lap and get comfy. You're going to be here a while."

An image formed in her head of her doing as Eric wanted, and even though her mind stalled and pushed back against the idea, her feet seemed to move of their own accord and took her directly to him.

"Are you sure about this?" she asked, and chewed on her bottom lip as she tried to work out the logistics of the situation.

Eric was tall, and while not exactly skinny, he was slim. His body was strong, she knew that. She'd felt his lean muscles when he'd pinned her against various walls over the past year and stolen kisses, and had seen his sinewy strength on full display when they'd come over to use the pool. But looking at the expanse of his thighs and comparing them to the width of her own, not to mention her soft belly, wide hips and flabby arse, gave Emily reason enough to pause.

"Do you need help getting into position?" Eric asked, one brow arching as he stared at her.

"No, Sir," she replied, running her hands over her hips, comparing their width with that of Eric's lap. "I'm just not sure I'll fit."

"There you go doing it again," Dane said with a sigh. "Putting yourself down."

"But—"

"But nothing," Eric said, the command in his voice silencing her. "Do you think we haven't thought of that already? That we haven't imagined what it would be like to see you over my knees with your head down and your arse up as I discipline you?"

"You better believe we've prepped for this," Dane added, then very deliberately ran his gaze over her nakedness and licked his lips. "The chance to see your pretty pussy dripping wet for us, peeking out between your sexy thighs. Mmm... I can't wait."

Emily inched a little closer to the bed. "I'm heavier than I look," she muttered, still frowning at Eric's lap.

"And I'm stronger than I look," he replied, then proved it by grabbing her around her waist and throwing her over his knees.

Chapter Ten

Struggling against his grip, she tried to get up but found she was too short. She couldn't successfully push herself back up using her hands, and the position she was in meant her toes didn't even touch the floor. And then she felt the pain of Eric's hand connecting with her backside. It was like a thousand bees all stinging her at once, and it sucked the air straight from her lungs, leaving her gasping and indignant.

But after the sting came a warmth that bloomed across her right arse cheek. The sensation was not an unpleasant one, but it was short-lived. Another stinging swat, this time on the left side of her arse made her cry out and renew her struggles. She swung her arm back in an attempt to cover herself and stop him from spanking her again but all she did was allow him to grab her wrist and pin her arm to her lower back, and earned her another smack.

"Why are we punishing you, Emily?" Eric's deep voice was like warmed honey. It wasn't fair. She wanted to hear that honeyed voice whisper dirty things in her ear, not ask her questions she didn't want to answer. She wanted to feel his big hands on her breasts, feel their warmth as he caressed her, not the heat of his stinging palm hitting her backside.

And where was Dane in all of this?

As if she'd summoned him with the thought, Dane suddenly appeared. Crouching down in front of her, he fisted his hand in her hair and lifted her head, and she was struck by how well the sting in her scalp complimented the heat spreading over her arse. How much it heightened her desire.

"Answer the question, baby," he said, his rich voice making her remember all the naughty things he'd teased her with for months. All the things she knew would be far more pleasurable than being punished.

Tears leaked from her eyes and blurred her vision. It was too much. Dane in front of her, coaxing her to speak, Eric's firm hands behind her, one gripping her wrist, the other gently rubbing, soothing the marks he'd already made. Her brain didn't know what to focus on. She couldn't think, so she shook her head and refused to answer.

A soft, dissatisfied sigh sounded above her followed by the jangling sound of a belt buckle and the cool touch of leather against her heated flesh. "Answer the question, Emily. Why are we punishing you?"

She tried to shake her head again but Dane tightened his grip, and then she screamed as the first lick of Eric's belt landed across her arse. Renewing her attempts to escape her situation, she kicked her legs and tried to throw herself sideways, away from the danger zone. But all she managed to do was earn another three stripes from the belt.

Dane brought his lips to her ear and whispered, "Why are we punishing you, baby? Answer the question."

Emily's tears were falling thick and fast, her nose was

blocked up and her pussy was soaking wet. How was that even possible? How was being spanked with a leather belt turning her on so fucking much? And why weren't they touching her?

She wanted them to touch her, she craved it, even as her brain revolted against the idea. It wasn't normal. She didn't know what to say. She didn't know what to feel. Everything kept getting more and more jumbled, more and more twisted around inside her.

What was the question again? Hadn't she already answered it? What was happening to her? What would have happened to her if they hadn't been at the drag race and taken her away? Is she still in danger? Why?

What did they want her to say?

Eric caressed her arse again, his big hand warm and sure. "It brings me no pleasure to punish you, kitten," he said, then slipped his hand between her buttocks and down to her pussy, slid a thick finger through her wetness. "Answer the question so we can end your punishment. Answer it so we can make you feel all better."

"Answer the question, baby. Answer it and we'll stop this," Dane said, then leaned into her ear again. "Answer the question and I'll eat your sweet cunt. I'll make you feel so fucking good, baby."

That zing of electricity was back, only now it was a throbbing pulse, a steady drumbeat drowning out any shred of rational thought she had left. Her body was primed and ready to explode, like a precision engine idling before a race. Just waiting for that igniting spark that would send her into overdrive.

Only that spark was nowhere to be seen. Eric removed his finger and went back to rubbing his palm over her aching backside, and Dane went back to pulling her hair, making it clear there would be no pleasure until she succumbed to the pain.

Until she gave them what they wanted.

"I can't think," she cried. "I don't know what you want me to say."

"Don't think," Eric said, and started spanking her again, a steady rhythm designed to drive her crazy. "You know the answer."

"Just say it, baby. Say what you feel."

"Don't think. Just feel."

"What is your heart telling you?" Dane said. "Answer the question."

"Why are we punishing you?"

"Because I gave up!" she screamed, then let her body sag, exhausted, as she sobbed. "I gave up. On you, on us... on me. I gave up."

The embarrassment of letting her truth spill free warmed her cheeks almost as much as Eric's spanking had warmed her arse. And she hadn't even realised it *was* her truth until she'd stopped overthinking and simply blurted out the thing she'd been trying to hide from everyone for what felt like forever.

She'd given up on herself. Had let herself succumb to the knowledge that she would never be anything other than David Berringer's daughter, office girl extraordinaire. The fact she could sell the shit out of any car put in front of her had somehow escaped her father's notice, and she wasn't even sure that was what she wanted to do with her life anymore anyway.

She was twenty-one years old and felt completely lost.

But before she could fall too deep into her despair, Emily found herself being helped up and repositioned in Eric's lap, her back pressed to his chest and her thick thighs spread wide. Wide enough for Dane to kneel between them.

"What are you doing?" she asked, sniffing back more tears.

"What I promised," he said gently. "You answered the question, so now I'm going to eat your sweet cunt and make you feel all better."

"Oh." She couldn't think of what else to say, except, "Why?"

"Because we're not giving up on you, kitten," Eric said, and swept her hair to one side. "We're not giving up on us." Then he nuzzled against her bare throat and licked and nibbled her skin, sent a sensual shiver right through her, down to her very soul.

Tilting her head to one side to allow him better access, Emily gasped when he cupped her breasts and pinched her nipples, rolled the hard little peaks between his fingers with just the right amount of pressure to make her mind go blank.

Then Dane slid his hands along the length of her thighs and used his thumbs to spread her pussy open, exposing her fully to his gaze.

"How wet is she?" Eric murmured against her neck.

A guttural groan came from between her legs. "Fucking soaked."

Emily knew she should be embarrassed, knew what they were doing to her was obscene, but she couldn't bring herself to care, especially when Dane flicked his tongue against her clit and sent her body into erotic overdrive. The man was relentless. They both were. Touching and teasing and licking and sucking, lavishing attention on every erotic nerve ending she owned.

Her body jolted as more of those electric zings pinballed around inside her, so much so that both Eric and Dane clamped their hands around her limbs to hold her in place for their continued debauchery.

Her brain didn't know what to focus on. It kept looping, kept spinning, spinning, spinning until she thought she'd go crazy. The pain in her nipples heightened the pleasure between her thighs. The lingering soreness and heat in her arse, was soothed by the wet, open-mouth kisses on her neck and shoulder.

And those zings. "Oh my God," she moaned. She was so close to coming. Every nerve in her body felt taut, ready to snap, and so help her if either one of them stopped what they were doing she would never speak to them ever again.

"That's it, kitten," Eric murmured against her throat. "That's our good girl. Don't think. Just feel." He bit her earlobe, eliciting another needy moan, then sucked the aching flesh between his soft lips. "Feel our love," he whispered in her ear. "Surrender to it. That's our girl. Such a good girl."

Dane chose that exact moment to slide two fingers deep inside her and curled them, applied pressure to just the right spot, then sucked her clit so hard that her orgasm didn't just manifest, it exploded out of her. Her back arched, her legs shook, and she screamed like a banshee as she surrendered to her men. Promised them over and over again to be their good girl, even as the aftershocks of her release slowly wore off and her body stilled, leaving her in a satiated heap.

A moment later, Dane was lifting her off his brother's lap and carrying her to the bathroom. The shower wasn't big enough for all three of them, but soon enough they were all cleaned up and ready for bed. Emily couldn't help noticing she was the only one still naked as they crawled under the covers, the brothers insisting on wearing their boxer briefs as they snuggled into her, as always, Eric at her front and Dane at her back, both of them sporting obvious erections.

"Make love to me," she whispered, brushing her hands over their cocks, revelling in their deep moans. "Please."

"Not tonight, baby," Dane said, removing her hand and adjusting himself so his cock nestled between her buttocks.

Emily pouted. "Am I still being punished?"

"No, kitten," Eric said, then chuckled and pressed a kiss to her forehead. "We are."

Chapter Eleven

Eric yawned and stretched the sleep from his body. He was still tired.

And rock hard.

Not surprising considering he'd spent the night next to the woman he was in love with and hadn't taken the time to lose himself in her sweet, soft body.

Not that he hadn't wanted to—he had, *desperately*—but he'd earned the pain of his abstinence.

Him and Dane both.

They'd known Emily was hiding something from them, had known for months, but they had no idea how deep her ennui truly went. And they'd only compounded her suffering with their disappearing act.

They had hurt their girl. Not intentionally, of course, but they'd suspected her listlessness had something to do with her position in the family business, had witnessed her slow retreat from family and friends, but they had never been able to get her to open up about it. Had never been able to break down that wall. And they hadn't been willing to push her too hard in case they pushed her away.

Until last night.

Eric hated that he'd caused their woman more pain, both physical and emotional. Hated how they'd had to keep her in the dark about their work. And the phone call he'd had to make before coming up to the bedroom had not gone well.

He and Dane were to front up at the station and give a full report of what happened at nine o'clock sharp.

Eric looked at the alarm clock beside the bed. It was almost six.

Turning on his side, he found Emily curled against Dane's chest, looking every bit like the kitten she was. He stroked her hair and absently rubbed the soft strands between his fingertips as the memory of the previous night replayed through his head.

He was a dirty fucker.

Even though he'd hated causing Emily pain, he'd loved seeing the acceptance and love in her eyes as she'd submitted to him. He'd hated her tears, but loved the capitulation behind them. Loathed using his belt on her flawless skin, but loved the marks it had left behind, marks that showed his possession. Showed she was his.

Lifting back the sheet, he exposed Emily's body. Her creamy skin begged for his attention, as did all of those sumptuous, sexy as fuck curves. The stripes on her arse had faded to almost nothing, but she would feel them for a while yet. For the rest of the day, whenever she sat down, she would be reminded of who she belonged to.

Reminded not to belittle herself.

We left her alone for too long.

As he lay there admiring his girl, goosebumps formed all over her exposed skin and she shivered, the early morning air still cool, even in the middle of a Queensland spring.

Snuggling closer, he stroked his hand down her body, smoothed away her chill, and in doing so earned himself a soft moan.

"Good morning," she murmured, and turned over to face him.

Dane rolled the other way. "Go back to sleep, baby," he groused. "Don't encourage him. It's too early to be awake."

Eric grinned. A morning person his brother was not.

"Good morning, kitten," he whispered, and pulled her closer, needing to feel the heat of her skin against his.

Within a heartbeat her legs were entwined with his, her head was tucked under his chin and her hands were stroking his chest, his arms, his back, then slipping inside his briefs and cupping his bare arse.

"You're wearing too many clothes," she said, her words punctuated by soft kisses against his neck.

"I guess you should take them off then," he replied, and almost laughed at how quickly his girl sprung into action, rolling him onto his back and relieving him of the only item of clothing he had on.

When she finished, she gingerly straddled his hips, as if reluctant to put her full weight on him again. Or possibly reluctant to put her full weight on her aching arsecheeks. Grinning up at her, he grabbed her hips and yanked her down, mashing her clit against the base of his cock and her arse against his thighs. The full contact made his grin vanish, his eyes roll back and he let out a lengthy groan. He couldn't help it. The feel of Emily's flesh moulding to his body was heaven, and the feel of her pussy on his aching cock, the heat, the wetness was fucking sublime, as evidenced by the droplets of come that wept from the tip of his dick and dripped onto his abdomen.

He was so engrossed in the feel of his girl on top of him

that he almost missed the look of hunger in her eyes as she stared at his cock. The way she licked her lips at the sight of those droplets on his body.

Tucking his hands behind his head, he said, "You want to suck my cock, kitten?"

Her bottom lip disappeared between her teeth and she nodded.

"What do we say?" he prodded, enjoying himself far too much for six o'clock on a Saturday morning.

Emily's hands splayed over his abdomen and a pale blush stained her cheeks. "Yes, sir," she said, a shy smile on her pretty mouth. "I want to suck your cock."

Movement from the other side of the bed momentarily stole his attention. Dane had rolled over and was staring at their girl with intense heat in his eyes, at the same time shoving his own briefs down his legs and kicking them off, sending them flying across the room.

Eric cocked one brow as he stared at his brother. "I thought you were tired."

Getting to his knees, he displayed his own hard cock for their girl's admiring gaze. "Not that fuckin' tired."

Emily giggled then dropped her gaze and gnawed at her lip. "I... I've never done this before, you know. With two guys at once."

Grabbing her wrists, Eric pulled her forwards until her breasts were squashed against his chest and her mouth was a hair's breadth from his. "We'll fuck you the same way we kiss you," he said, fisting one hand in her hair. "Any way you want." Then he slammed their mouths together and swallowed her surprised squeak, ravished her mouth with the same passion he would soon devote to her pussy.

When he finally eased her back, her face was flushed

and her eyes hooded. He'd missed that, the blissed out expression she always wore after kissing her.

Eric remembered the first time he and Dane had kissed her, not long after they'd met. They'd been walking through the Queen Street Mall when they'd spotted her, standing in line for ice cream, wearing white sneakers, an oversized white T-shirt, and a pair of pink denim shorty-shorts that hugged her voluptuous arse like a second skin.

His trousers had become uncomfortably tight the moment he'd seen her and his whole body had itched with the need to touch her, to discover if her skin was as soft as he'd imagined, if she smelled as good as he'd remembered.

As they'd approached her, he'd noticed two school girls in line behind her, tall, thin girls, giggling and make rude gestures, making fun of their girl's generous curves. He'd also seen the strain on Emily's face as she'd tried to ignore the ignorant little twats, seen the way her fingers tightened around the strap of her handbag, almost as if she was imagining wringing their necks.

He hadn't needed to say anything to his brother—they'd always been on the same page where Emily was concerned —and before he could think twice, he was standing beside her, cupping her cheek and lifting her face to his. "Sorry we're late, kitten." Then he'd kissed her like his life depended on it.

"Did you miss us?" Dane had asked, then he too had kissed her deeply. So deeply in fact, the ice cream vendor had to clear her throat to get their attention. "Order anything you want, baby. Our treat."

"Huh?" It had taken her a moment to realise they were talking about the ice cream, to shake off her sensual stupor. "Oh, um... one scoop of pistachio, and ah... one scoop of honey caramel macadamia. Please." Then she'd stared up at them in turn, returned their smiles and blushed the prettiest shade of pink. "Hi."

Behind them, the two girls had turned to stone, their mouths hanging open, their eyes wide and brimming with confusion. He supposed it wasn't everyday they saw a police officer pash a woman in broad daylight, let alone two officers pashing the same woman.

He still couldn't believe they'd gotten away with doing that, considering there always seemed to be some busy-body ready to dob in a copper for unseemly conduct.

But a passionate kiss was the least unseemly thing he had planned for Emily that morning.

Chapter Twelve

Easing his hand from her hair, Eric stroked it down her back until it rested on her arse, then gave it a gentle squeeze. He smirked at her quiet whimper. "Want me to kiss it better?"

Emily snorted. "Did you really just ask me if I want you to kiss my arse?"

He chuckled at her sass then spanked her, eliciting another groan, another wiggle of her hips that pushed her cunt against his cock and sent a shot of pure pleasure up his spine. "I can kiss your arse if you like," he said, "but I'd rather eat your pussy."

That sweet blush bloomed over her cheeks again and she bit her lip and nodded. "Yes, please."

"On your feet, baby," Dane instructed, then helped her get in position, straddling Eric's head, facing his feet.

"Are you sure he won't suffocate?"

"Meh." He could hear the shrug in his brother's voice. "If he dies, he dies."

"That's not very reassuring," she grumbled, hovering over him, denying him his prize.

"Sounds like someone needs another reminder about who's in charge," Eric said, then gripped her thighs in both hands and forced her body down over his face.

Sinking his teeth into her fleshy thigh, he revelled in her yelp, then soothed the ache with his tongue. Over and over he did that, avoiding her pussy, driving the anticipation higher until she relaxed into position, wrapped her delicate fingers around his cock and took him into her mouth.

The warmth of her body enveloped him, her thick thighs the most luxurious pillows he'd ever rested his head on. Her body pressed along his, the softest of blankets. But her mouth was a different kind of heat, wet and greedy and all consuming. And when she slid her tongue along the sensitive underside of his shaft, and flicked it around the head of his cock, his brain turned to mush.

"*Fuuuck*," he breathed, then reciprocated the action, matched her enthusiasm and went to town on her cunt.

"Fuck, yes," Dane growled from somewhere beyond them, then the bed dipped and moved as his brother joined them. Suddenly Emily's head has yanked off his cock, and Eric could hear Dane's breathing change. His little brother had stolen his prize for himself.

He would call him a selfish prick but that wasn't the way they worked.

What was his, was theirs, and he knew Dane felt the same.

Always had, always would.

"That's it, baby. Suck my cock. Such a good girl." Then he heard a wet pop and her mouth was back on him. "Such a good girl," Dane crooned. "Suck his cock, Emily. Make him come."

Eric flicked his tongue against Emily's clit then sucked it between his lips. He pinched and he bit and he soothed.

He stroked and he licked and he teased until her body quivered and tightened, until her hips bucked and she fucked his face and yelled his name.

"Eric, fuck yes!"

He continued licking and sucking until she started to squirm, until the sweetness that was Emily Berringer stopped running down his chin.

"Get on your back, baby." Dane helped manoeuvre their girl into position once more then tossed Eric a condom. "Age before beauty," he said with a wink, then went back to devouring Emily with his eyes, stroking her ankle, her leg, with loving affection.

"We're going to fuck you now," Eric said. Crawling over the top of her, he propped himself up on his arms and stared down at her, drank in her pretty blue eyes and flushed skin, memorised the plump curve of her shy smile, the faint pattern of freckles on her cheeks. "Is that okay?"

Emily nodded enthusiastically.

"Say it," Dane demanded, his voice heavy with lust.

Her throat bobbed and she wet her lips as her gaze danced between them. "Yes, I want you to fuck me. Both of you. I want that very much."

Eric didn't need to hear another word. He fisted one hand around his cock and guided himself home, sank into Emily's willing body to the hilt then threw back his head and groaned. "So fucking good."

When he looked down at her again, her eyes were hooded and her teeth held her bottom lip hostage. Using his thumb, he freed her lip then bent his head and took her mouth again, only softer, less urgent. He let himself indulge in the teasing way she plucked at his lips with her own, the way her tongue slow-danced with his, and all while he moved inside her.

While he made love to her.

Emily buried her face in the crook of his neck, nipped and sucked on his skin. Moaned his name and wrapped herself around him. He was lost in her, in the feel of her wet heat, the smell of skin. Then she raked her fingernails across his arse, leaving stinging trails in their wake and spurring him to fuck her faster. Harder.

Moving to his knees, Eric gripped Emily under her thighs and pulled her to him, slammed their bodies together over and over as he fucked her with bruising need.

But as intense as their passion was, it wasn't enough to keep her focus completely on him. Her gaze drifted to Dane, hungry, pleading, before coming back to him, as if silently asking his permission to be naughty. She wasn't to know his brother was only being cautious, this being her first time fucking them.

"You're sure?"

"Yes. Very sure."

He grinned at her and nodded. Who was he to deny her anything? "Dane, give our girl something to suck on."

His brother rejoined them on the bed and kneeled by Emily's head, and she needed no prodding to take him in her mouth again. In fact she seemed to relish it.

"Naughty girl."

She threw him a cheeky smile, at least she tried to. He imagined it wasn't easy, smiling with a cock down your throat, but the smile didn't last. As Eric pounded into her, he felt her body tighten, felt her slick heat splash him with every thrust of his hips. Dane eased back and gave her room, then pumped his cock in his fist, and they both watched in awe as Emily's body convulsed with her second orgasm, as her back arched and her toes curled and her hands fisted in the sheets.

"Oh my God. Yes. YES!"

The sight of their woman lost in her passion was enough to push Eric over the edge. He'd fought the urge to come for long enough and couldn't hold it back anymore. Locking eyes with his girl, he let himself go, let his orgasm take hold and rode his own wave of ecstasy. Slammed his hips home so hard she'd be sure to feel it for days.

And just as he sat back, panting and satiated, still buried deep inside Emily, Dane shot his load over her breasts then fed her the tip of his dick, groaned as she licked him clean.

"I fucking love you, baby," Dane said, then leaned down and kissed her.

"I love you, too," she replied, her voice soft and languid. Then she looked at Eric and smiled. *So beautiful.* "And you. I love you, too."

Eric didn't answer. He eased himself out of her and disposed of the condom, then came back to the bed and hauled Emily into his lap. "So, now that you've had a little taste of what it truly means to be ours, are you sure you still want this?" He tucked a strand of her sweat-slicked hair behind her ear. "Are you sure you still want us?"

Emily stared at him like he'd just asked her the dumbest question in the history of dumb questions, then asked one of her own. "Are you sure you still want me?"

"Of course we want you," he said. "*I* want you. I love you, Emily."

"Good," she said, a goofy smile blooming on her face. "Now shut up and kiss me."

After kissing each of them in turn, Dane climbed off the bed. "Why don't you two shower and get dressed," he said. "I'll make coffee."

Emily cocked one brow as she watched Dane leave, her gaze glued to his arse. "He's going to make coffee naked?"

Eric nodded. "He usually does."

"Um... does he know about the security cameras Teddy set up last month?"

Eric's eyes widened at the news, then he shook his head and laughed. Neither of them had known. "Nope."

Emily slipped off his lap and moved to follow his brother, to protect him in her own way. "Shouldn't we—"

"Tell him?" He laughed again and grabbed her wrist, pulled her back and kissed her until she softened in his arms. "Where's the fun in that?"

Chapter Thirteen

By the time Dane and Eric dropped Emily off at work and got to the station for their briefing, Dane wanted to hit something. Or someone. Thankfully his older brother was the calmer of the two, and he knew Eric would help him keep his cool.

He hated this undercover bullshit. Hated that it took them away from Emily, that it put her in danger. Hated that if they fucked this up it could—probably would—fuck up their futures within the service.

The rank of Detective.

That was their end goal.

They'd always loved solving puzzles, loved helping people, and becoming detectives ticked both boxes. And when they'd been approached about helping out with the investigation into Shane Spencer and his little drag racing club, they were promised it would help them reach their goal. That being involved in ops like this one was a good way to get noticed, a nice feather in their caps for their resumes. But when they had made it known they were uncomfortable with the undercover side of things, they'd been requisitioned anyway.

Like a piece of fucking equipment.

The only thing keeping Dane's temper in check when they entered the building was the memory of Emily's sweet mouth wrapped around his dick, sucking on him like he was her favourite treat. That and the memory of her hot cunt, when he'd been buried between her soft thighs and eating his goddamn fill of her.

"Fuck," he groaned and adjusted himself, but not discreetly enough to avoid his brother's notice.

Eric smirked at him. "Stop thinking about Emily. Getting a hard-on won't win you any favours with this bloke."

"I don't care about winning favours. I just want to go back to doing our real jobs. And I don't like that we left Em at the dealership without protection. They know she works there."

His brother's expression twisted with concern. "I don't like it either, but she was right. They have security cameras everywhere and a guard on duty. And Teddy is there today."

"So?"

"So we already know the lengths the convict will go to, to protect his family." He snorted. "I would not want to be in Spencer's shoes if he *does* prove dumb enough to show up unannounced." Eric stopped and gripped Dane's shoulder, gave it a reassuring squeeze. "Our girl is protected, so how about we get our reports written up before we get called into the principal's office?"

They found their desks and got to work, filled out the required reports, noting everything that had happened at the drag race, before and after Emily's arrival, including the fact there hadn't been an actual race due to the cops being called.

He'd just finished going over his report one last time, when a large man in a cheap suit leaned against his desk. Dane gritted his teeth. The very last thing he needed was this guy trying to get a rise out of him.

"What do you want, Travis?"

"Me and the guys in homicide have a question," he said, then paused to sip his coffee out of a mug with World's Best Detective printed on the side of it. Dane only just managed to stop himself from rolling his eyes. The chances of Travis being the world's best detective were as small as the idiot's dick. "When you and your brother fuck a woman, do you take turns, or is it just a free for all?" He leaned closer, lowered his voice. "Just between you and me, do the two of you ever, you know, cross swords?"

Dane took the fact he wasn't punching the walking shit-stain in the face as a sign of personal growth. *Eric will be so proud.* But he also knew how rumours started and he'd be damned if he let this fuckwit taint his and Eric's relation-ship with Emily.

If anyone was going to be the object of ridicule, it wasn't going to be them. Travis was a bully, and the best way to deal with a bully was to push them into the spotlight.

Raising his voice just enough to get noticed, Dane said, "Are you seriously asking me if I fuck my brother? What the hell is wrong with you, man?"

Travis took a step back from Dane's desk, his face flushed red. "Hey, now that—"

"Hey, Eric."

The look on his brother's face told him he'd already heard what was going on, but he played along all the same. "What?"

"Travis wants to know if we fuck each other."

Eric stared at Travis with disgust. "Seriously? You homicide guys are fucked in the head."

Other officers started sticking their heads out from behind their computers, grinning and whispering, which only flustered Travis more. "Now listen here," he said, waving his hand about and sloshing coffee out of his mug. "I've—"

"What the bloody hell is going on out here?"

Senior Sargeant Jody Walker appeared behind Travis, her permascowl fixed firmly in place and her hands clasped behind her back. She was their father's younger sister, and out of uniform they called her Aunty Jo, but as the senior officer in charge of the station, they were just as terrified of her as everyone else.

"Well?" she demanded. "Who wants to go first?" When no one spoke up, she nodded. "That's what I thought." Then she turned on Travis and pointed to the spilled coffee. "Clean that mess up."

Travis smiled tightly and smoothed down his necktie. "Yes, ma'am."

"Good. Everyone else, get back to work," she said, then pointed at Dane and his brother. "You two, my office. Now."

They entered the office to find the man in charge of the operation, and another man they didn't know, staring at them with obvious irritation.

Jo introduced everyone then took her seat and invited everyone else to do the same. "So—"

"What the fuck happened last night?"

"Detective Bryant, I urge you to control yourself," Jo said.

"Control myself? They're lucky I don't put my boot through their skulls after the mess they caused."

"The mess *we* caused?" Dane said. He was half out of his chair when Eric caught his shoulder and dragged him back down.

"Thank God Detective Cross was acting as your shadow last night and called in the cavalry."

"Yes, well done," Eric drawled, injecting a healthy dose of sarcasm into his usual stoic charm. "Of course, all you managed to do was scatter the cockroaches, and made it just that little bit harder to do our job."

"Are you fucking kidding me?" Bryant raged. "Your job was to keep an eye on the drug dealers these damn races keep attracting. Not hook up with a car slut and get yourself into a fight with Shane fucking Spencer. Is it true you pulled your weapons?"

Dane's grip tightened on the arms of his chair until his knuckles blanched. "Did you just call Emily a slut?" he growled through gritted teeth.

"Answer the question, Senior Constable."

"Wait," Jo said, holding up her hand, then stared at Dane and Eric. "Did you say Emily? As in *Emily*, Emily?"

He and Eric nodded. "Yes."

"Who cares what her fucking name is?"

"Detective Bryant," Jo barked, furious authority bleeding out of her as she glared at the man. "The young woman in question is a dear family friend, and her brother is engaged to my niece. If you call her by anything other than her name again, I will have you written up for conduct unbecoming. Do you understand me?"

Bryant's mouth tightened and he rolled his shoulders. "Yes, ma'am. I apologise. It won't happen again."

"It better not. Now, first things first. Is Emily all right?"

Nodding, Dane released a slow breath and relaxed his grip on the chair, flexed his fingers to get the blood flowing again. "Yeah, she's safe."

"For now," Cross said, folding his arms over his chest. "Spencer isn't going to let her get away with humiliating him like she did." Then he chuckled. "Not that it wasn't fucking spectacular to watch that little shit get taken down a few pegs. Especially by a woman," he added, then sent him and Eric a nod of approval. Not that they needed or even wanted his approval.

Jo frowned at them. "Why was she even there? Emily has never struck me as the type of woman to go looking for trouble."

Dane shared a look with Eric, then sighed. "She was on a date," he said. "With Matthew Spencer, of all people. She thought they were going to Willowbank but the little shit took her there instead."

Their aunt's frown deepened. "But I thought you two and her were... you know."

"We were taking it slow," Eric said. "Too slow, apparently. And then we got brought in on this and couldn't tell her anything about it, so...."

"So she thought you weren't interested anymore and went out with someone else. Got it." Jo laughed but there was no humour in it. "And now she's stuck in the middle of this mess."

"We were trying to get her out of there as quietly as possible, but things didn't exactly go to plan. Shane noticed her and liked what he saw."

"And was that before or after she hit his brother?" Jo asked, flicking through the reports in front of her.

"After," Dane said. "She hit Matthew because he called

her a slut." He faced Detective Bryant and grinned with grim satisfaction. "Would you like to meet her?"

The older man snorted and shook his head but wisely kept his mouth shut, which was a good thing. Dane wasn't sure he could listen to any more of the man's crap without getting himself into serious trouble.

"Well, it looks like you need a new plan, gentlemen. Any suggestions?"

"I could think of a few," Bryant grumbled.

"Before I put forward my suggestion, I have a question," Cross said. "If Emily had raced Spencer last night, could she have won?"

"That's why you called it in?" Dane said. "You didn't think she could win?"

Cross's brow shot up and he stared at them like they were idiots. "I called it in because the situation was escalating out of your control. But now I'm curious. Did she have a chance? Could she have beaten him?"

Now it was their turn to stare at Cross like he was the idiot. Dane laughed. "Yeah, she could have."

"Bullshit," Bryant said. "No one beats Spencer. That's how he keeps getting away with this shit."

"Emily was taught how to race by her brother," Eric said, "and to this day he is the only person she can't beat."

"And who's her brother?" Cross asked.

"Edward Berringer," Jo supplied.

"Why do I know that name?" Bryant asked.

"About ten years ago he gave evidence that helped your team take down the biggest car theft ring in South East Queensland," she said. "He also did a six month stretch for, among other things, the property damage he caused when he led the police on a high speed chase through Brisbane.

The chase that caught the ringleader's daughter and her top drivers."

Cross laughed and nodded. "I remember him. Fuck me. Emily is Emily Berringer. Jesus, no wonder she was so cocky." He stared at Dane and Eric with a considering look. "You really think she can do it, don't you? You think she can beat him."

"That's your suggestion?" Bryant demanded. "To get a civilian involved. No. Not happening."

"Finally, we agree on something," Dane said.

Eric turned to face him, his expression as serious as it had ever been, which was saying a lot considering Eric wasn't known for his lighter side. "You said it yourself last night, Dane. Emily may not have a choice."

"No. We keep her out of it. We keep her safe."

"That's not what you said last night," Eric reminded him.

"Yeah, well, I've changed my mind, okay. I made a judgement call based on the information we had at the time. But she's been removed from the situation now. Why put her back in it?" He shook his head and rubbed at the ache in the centre of his chest. "I don't want her anywhere near it. I don't want her anywhere near him."

"You think I do?" Eric scowled. "Dane, she won't be safe until Shane Spencer is put away. Detective Cross is right, she humiliated him. He's not going to forget that. And now that everyone is on the same page again, it really doesn't matter if she wins or not, as long as we catch him in the act." His brother pinned the other men with a glare. "Because we will catch him, right?"

"If we can find out where the next meet is."

Bryant rubbed his chin. "You said she showed up last night with Matthew Spencer? Any chance she has his contact info? Maybe we can use him to find out where tonight's race is."

Much to Dane's chagrin, Eric agreed, and they all spent the next two hours hammering out the details of their plan and working out contingencies for every possible outcome. They also gave detailed accounts of the drug deals they'd witnessed, plus the sale of counterfeit car parts, and at least one incidence of prostitution, just for good measure.

It seemed Shane Spencer was a regular entrepreneur.

Once everything was settled, Dane looked at his brother and forced a smile. "Great. So. Who wants to tell Emily the plan?"

Eric pulled a coin out of his pocket, flipped it in the air and called it. "Heads."

The coin landed in his brother's palm, tails side up. "Fuck."

Chapter Fourteen

Emily shoved her hands in her pockets and paced from one end of the dealership to the other, trying her best not to freak out.

When the guys had dropped her off at work, they'd been worried for her safety. Dane especially had not wanted to leave her alone. They had insisted on coming inside and checking everything out, and even held an in-depth conversation with her brother about everything that was going on, which had been... interesting.

She had completely forgotten that Teddy was even on the Saturday roster, and to say he was furious was the understatement of the century, although she wasn't sure which part of the story irritated him more. The fact she'd caught the attention of someone like Shane Spencer, or the fact she'd spent the night with Eric and Dane.

Either way, it was a miracle the guys had left in one piece.

And as soon as they were gone, she had received the chewing out to end all chewing outs from her over-protective big brother. And it had felt worse than anything her parents could have said, because Teddy had spoken from experience.

Her guilt had threatened to overwhelm her, until he'd pulled her into his arms and squeezed her so tightly she'd thought her ribs might burst. That's when she'd realised her brother's anger had come from a place of fear.

That he was scared for her.

Join the club.

Emily supposed Teddy had hoped she would have learned from his mistakes. Not that she had put herself in that position on purpose, and not that she would ever be able to see what had happened as a mistake. Not when it had led her back to Eric and Dane and the passion they had shared.

She would never regret that.

By the time her men had returned with lunch—from her favourite sushi place, no less—Teddy had *almost* accepted the fact their relationship went beyond the physical, that they were in love. Almost.

He'd been staring daggers at them ever since they'd returned from their meeting with their superiors.

Of course, it hadn't helped when Dane had relayed The Plan, which essentially boiled down to:

- Emily race psychopath.
- Emily beat psychopath.
- Police arrest everyone at the finish line.
- Eric and Dane take Emily home and fuck her brains out.

Although she was pretty sure that last point wasn't an

official part of The Plan, and more likely Dane needing to express his frustration at how vehemently he opposed The Plan.

Considering he wasn't opposed to her racing Shane the night before, he had certainly changed his tune. But then, so had she. Sure, it had seemed like the right thing to do at the time, but now, many, *many* hours later, she saw her actions for what they truly were.

Completely insane.

And it was that insanity that her boyfriends wanted her to repeat. Well, not them. Not really. They had both made it perfectly clear they would rather walk over red hot coals than put her in danger again, but she could see their point and that of their superiors. If they wanted to get the Spencer brothers and their drug dealing friends off the streets, they needed to think outside the box.

Even so, Dane reminded her that she didn't have to go through with it. She was a civilian. They couldn't make her do it, but then Eric reminded her that she'd made a fool out of a crazy person who wasn't big on forgiveness.

And that person was walking towards her with all the swagger of a lion in a butcher's shop. He saw her as easy prey.

And that really pissed her off.

Staring Shane down as he approached, Emily resisted the urge to shake the nervous tension from her hands and reminded herself that Eric, Dane, Teddy, and three other undercover officers posing as customers and staff were in the store with her. All of them willing and able to help her should she need it.

Still, she could have gone the rest of her life never seeing this douchebag again and would have been very happy to do so. But earlier, when she'd sent the text message to his brother asking for the details of the next race, she'd known there was a chance he would come looking for her. As much as she loved being proven right, this was one case she would have loved to have gotten it wrong.

Thanking that powers that be that she'd worn trousers and a very modest blouse— nothing even remotely revealing for Shane to ogle—Emily crossed her arms and scowled at him as he ran his hand over the vintage BMW 328 they had on display in the showroom. Her father always said it was a reminder of quality workmanship and design. In reality it was a sales ploy to make rich arseholes feel like a part of motoring history.

"Nice car," Shane said. "Sexy curves."

Emily refused to bite. "Why are you here?"

Shane smiled, and again she was struck by how seductive he looked. It really was no wonder why women fell for bad men. When the outside looked so good, it was easy to imagine the inside looked the same. "You wanted to know where the next race was, didn't you?"

"You could have texted."

"Where's the fun in that?"

"Fun?" She snorted. "Fun will be when I win your ride, dismantle it and sell it off for scrap."

"Scrap? That's cute." He moved closer. "You're cute." His gaze narrowed. "But you have an attitude, and when you lose, that's the first thing I'm gunna to fuck out of you." Then he reached out to touch her, but she slapped his hand away.

"Don't touch me," she snarled, a sliver of fear creeping up her spine, causing goosebumps to form all over her.

Shane held up his hands in surrender and chuckled. "Okay. I won't touch you. Yet. But when you lose our race—

and you will lose—I'm gunna touch you as much as I want, in any way I want. And maybe,"—he leaned closer, lowered his voice—"I'll let my brother touch you too, since you're into that sort of thing."

Fury stumbled over fear as Emily stared at the shithead. "Fuck you!"

His smile broadened, taunted her, but before he could say anything else that might upset her, Eric and Dane marched towards them looking ready to murder him.

"What the fuck do you want?" Dane demanded, manoeuvring Emily behind him and Eric, forming a protective wall in front of her.

"Don't shoot the messenger," Shane said, then reached into his pocket and pulled out a piece of paper. "Just delivering the details for tonight's meet." He dragged his teeth over his bottom lip and stared directly at Emily. "And reminding myself of what I'm winning."

Dane took a step forwards but Eric clamped his hand on his brother's shoulder and stopped him. "You won't win. She will *never* be yours."

He chuckled. "We'll see." Then he tipped his chin at her. "Won't we, cutie?"

"In case you didn't hear me the last time, let me say it again. Ew."

A muscle ticked in his cheek but he quickly smiled again to cover it. "I love it when you play hard to get." Then he tried handing the piece of paper to Emily but Eric snatched it out of his hand. "See you tonight, cutie," Shane said, then winked, but there was nothing playful about the action. "And don't forget to bring your boyfriends. I want them to watch when I humiliate you." Then he turned and walked away, casually waving one hand in the air as if they were the oldest of friends.

Emily flipped him off.

As soon as Shane was out of sight, Teddy joined them, his face as thunderous as her men. Eric read the note. "We have a time and a place," he said, then pulled out his phone. "Excuse me for a moment, kitten."

Eric left to make his call, the undercover cops around the store filing out after him, but Dane stayed and pulled her into a hug, tucked her head beneath his chin and held her close. "You don't have to do this, Em," he told her again. "Not if you don't want to."

"He's right," Teddy said. "You don't owe anyone anything."

She buried her face in her Dane's chest and breathed him in. Let his masculine scent wrap around her. "I know," she said, her stomach churning with a caustic combination of fear, anger and anticipation.

"Then let the cops handle this."

"We just want to keep you safe, baby."

"And I appreciate that." She leaned back and pressed a fist to her mouth, fought the urge to vomit, then took a deep breath and slowly let it out. She shook her head. "It was my own stupidity that got us into this mess, and while I don't particularly *want* to race Shane, I think doing this, doing my part, matters." She stroked Dane's cheek, adored the way he leaned into her touch, as if he couldn't get enough of it, of her. "I am so lucky. I am surrounded by people who want to protect me. People who love me, who would miss me if I ever—" She cut off the thought. "But what about the next person he goes after? They may not be that lucky." She leaned into him again, sought out his strength. "I don't know how much help I can be, but I want to try."

She felt Dane's heavy sigh through his chest. "And by

try you mean scaring the shit out of us all by driving through suburbia at insane speeds."

She pulled back again and grinned up at him. "Whatever helps."

Eric returned a moment later, slung his arm around her waist and pressed a kiss to her temple. "Everyone has been notified."

Teddy snorted. "And just like that everyone's on board?" He stared at them like they were all nuts, then shook his head. "Fuck me dead," he muttered. "You know what? Fine. Emily is an adult and can make her own adult decisions, but"—he drilled a finger into Eric's chest—"if anything happens to her—*anything*—I swear to God not even the love I have for your sister will save you."

"Aye, aye, convict," Dane said, throwing him a mock salute.

Emily jabbed her elbow into his ribs. "What did I say about calling him convict?"

Dane didn't look even remotely sorry, but apologised anyway. "Sorry, baby. Force of habit."

Her brother's eyes narrowed as he stared at them for a moment longer, then he shook his head, muttered, "For fuck's sake," under his breath, then left to see to the customer that had entered the store.

"So what do we do now?" Emily asked, allowing Eric to pull her into a hug. "Just go about our day like normal?"

"Cross said to relax and get some rest. We have a busy night ahead of us."

"I'm too wired to rest," Emily grumbled.

"Is that so?" Eric said. "In that case, how would you feel about going on a date instead?"

"A date?" Emily repeated, her heartrate kicking it up a notch at the thought of what a real date with the Walker brothers would entail. "Not just another family barbeque but a proper, *proper* date?" No more sneaking around? No more hiding her affection? Any thought of getting rest, no matter how small, was crushed under the weight of her excitement at getting to spend quality time with her men. In public. "Where are we going and when do we leave?"

Chapter Fifteen

The blindfold over Emily's eyes was soft, but it blocked everything. No sight, no light, nothing was getting through the thick black fabric. She bit her lip to hold in a nervous giggle as Eric and Dane led her... somewhere.

They'd left the dealership not long after Shane's visit, and gone home to shower and change. She'd tried multiple times to engage them in sexy fun times, but to her continuing frustration, they'd rebuffed her advances each and every time.

"We need to keep our edge, baby," Dane had told her.

At which point she had deliberately dropped her towel so they could see exactly what they were passing up. "And not fucking me keeps you on edge?"

Eric had grunted and adjusted his cock in his jeans. "You have no fucking idea."

Then the brothers had grabbed her, Dane pinning her arms behind her back, and Eric latching one hand around her throat while using the other to torment her. He'd thrust two fingers deep inside her pussy then used his thumb to not quite touch her clit, just rubbed slow circles around and around the sensitive little nub until her knees grew weak and she was begging them to fuck her.

"No sex. Not yet," Eric had growled, his gaze blazing with longing and lust. "So unless you want us to keep *you* on edge for the next few hours, I suggest you behave yourself, kitten."

Emily had groaned. She'd almost come from the salacious suggestion alone, but the feel of them touching her, of being trapped between her men and feeling their hard lengths pressing into her, knowing they wanted her as much as she wanted them just ramped up her anticipation for later, for the final step in The Plan.

She also suspected the whole blindfold thing was just another way to keep her on edge. They were being ridiculously secretive.

Listening for clues as to where they might be wasn't particularly helpful. The door leading into the building sounded pretty normal, as did the way her shoes sounded on the carpeted flooring. The smell was familiar to her but she couldn't quite put her finger on it—hotdogs, maybe?— and the decades old music sounded distant and hollow, like it was coming from a large, empty room.

"Have you guessed yet?" Dane asked, his warm breath brushing against her ear.

"Um... bowling alley?" But she didn't think that was quite right.

When the boys lifted the blindfold, Emily had to raise her hand to block the sudden barrage of lights. Flashing, twinkling lights, twirling in time with the music. Suddenly Eric was standing in front of her, using his body to block the worst of it.

"Let your eyes adjust," he said. "There's no rush."

So she took a moment and did as Eric suggested, while surreptitiously taking in her surroundings and discovering they were in a roller skating rink.

A very empty roller skating rink.

So much for her public displays of affection.

"You look annoyed," Dane said, casting a worried glance at Eric. "Why is she annoyed?"

Emily tried to school her features into something more neutral, but she'd never been very good at hiding her feelings. Her face screamed things she would never have to courage to say out loud.

Eric gripped her chin and made her look at him. "What's going on, kitten? Why are you upset?"

She started to say, "I'm not upset," but Eric's hand slipped from her chin to her throat and squeezed just enough to make her think twice about lying to him.

"Don't hide from us, baby. Talk to us."

She hated being so easy to read. And both of her men were damn good at it.

Closing her eyes, she took a moment to breathe, to organise her thoughts. Then she lifted her chin and stared at them head on. "Are you ashamed of me?"

"What?" Their shocked expressions was some consolation at least, but she'd seen good acting before. "No, we're not ashamed of you. Why would you think that?"

"Because you said you were taking me on a real date. I assumed that meant somewhere public. I was wrong."

Eric relaxed and a small grin tugged at one corner of his mouth. "You think we're hiding you." He shook his head. "We're not."

Emily gestured to the empty rink. "You'll have to forgive me for thinking otherwise. Especially since—"

She bit off what she was going to say, the reminder of past humiliations still living rent free in her head. Images of a certain boy laughing at her when she'd dared to ask him why they never went out with his friends, why he never came over when her family was home. When he'd confirmed her worst fears and told her she wasn't his girlfriend, that he would never date someone who looked like her. That he'd been told fat girls were more fun in bed, and was surprised to find out it was true. And yeah, that shithead had a lot of fun at her expense.

"Since it wouldn't be the first time?"

"Since Billy Houghton did the same thing?"

Her narrowed gaze snapped to Eric's then Dane's. "How do you know about him?"

"We're cops," Dane said, pressing himself against her back and nuzzling her earlobe. "We know things."

"And did you really think we wouldn't look into your past boyfriends after you told us you hadn't dated anyone in almost three years." Eric's deep blue gaze was as mesmerising as the commanding tone in his velvety voice. "Why would a smart, funny, gorgeous woman remove herself from the dating scene unless she'd been hurt by someone?"

Emily opened her mouth to say something but nothing came out, her mind blank of all conscious thought because Dane chose that exact moment to grab her arsecheeks and squeeze them hard, hard enough to force her onto her toes and try to escape the fresh ache he was causing.

"Do you need a reminder of our conversation last night?" he said.

No one calls our girl names. Especially not our girl.

"You're ours, Emily," Eric said, "and we protect what's ours."

"Which is why we're here early," Dane chimed in, and gave her a final swat on her aching backside before moving away.

"What do you mean?" she asked, gingerly rubbing her butt.

Eric pressed a firm kiss to her lips then released her, stepped back and offered her his hand. "Come with us and we'll show you."

Tentatively, she took his hand and let him lead her over to the skate desk, where three pairs of skates were already lined up. "I don't understand what's happening," she said, but she still took the skates and began putting them on.

"There's a roller disco here tonight," Dane said. "We know the owner. He let us in early so we could get in some practice."

Her lips pressed together and she rolled her eyes. "So I don't embarrass you when I fall flat on my face, you mean."

Dane grinned. "I think someone wants another spanking."

"I do not," she said, then stood up and tested her balance with the heavy skates on her feet. Then her left foot rolled forward unexpectedly and she fought to stay upright. Her mouth twisted to one side. "I don't know about this." Her skating ability was not great.

"Come here, kitten."

Emily immediately covered her backside with both hands, the speed of her movement almost landing her back on the chair, and shook her head. "I don't want another spanking," she whined.

Eric chuckled. "No spanking. I promise. Now, come here." He stood confidently with his skates on and held out hands out towards her. His movements were so smooth and graceful, and made her feel even more out of place. Even so, she attempted to do as he'd asked, awkwardly half skating, half walking towards him.

"Good girl," he said, smiling at her without even a hint of derision or disgust, and some small part of the tension she'd been holding on to since they'd removed the blindfold melted away.

"You know, I'm really more of an armchair athlete," she said, watching her feet, as if that would grant her magical skating powers. "I'm much better at cheering on others."

But her men disagreed. Taking her hands in theirs, they led her out onto the rink and slowly began circling the concrete structure, holding her upright and stopping her from making a complete fool of herself.

Eric gave her gentle instruction and Dane encouraged her to be bold, and soon she was skating all by herself. Well... almost. The guys were never more than a foot away from her, ready to help her whenever she needed them.

Even in something as simple as this, they protected her.

"How are you two so good at this? I mean, Karen, yeah, I get it. But you two?"

Their sister Karen was a roller derby girl, a member of the B52 Bombshells, and Emily loved going to her bouts and cheering her on from the stands, but she never would have guessed her men were so swift of foot on eight wheels.

"Who do you think taught Kiki?" Dane laughed, and started skating backwards.

"Show off."

"A lot of our misspent youth was spent right here," Eric said. "Our mum had buggered off to parts unknown with her not-so-secret side-piece, and Dad had to work all the time, so we came here."

"Every weekend, every school holiday," Dane added.

"Our first jobs were here too, cleaning toilets and sanitising skates."

Emily smiled at the thought of her men doing anything other than being cops. "That sounds—"

"Gross?" Dane said. "Because it was."

"I was going to say awesome, but yeah,"—she screwed up her nose—"I guess cleaning foot funk out of skates would be kinda gross."

As they continued talking, Emily found her rhythm, learned to relax into the movements, when to push and when to glide, and she began to appreciate the music and took in the full scope of their surroundings.

A large mirror ball hung over the centre of the rink, reflecting the strobe lights and casting rainbows all over the floor and walls, and brightly coloured banners were hung up all over the place, announcing vendors and sponsors for the disco. It was all so bright and fun and silly. A million miles away from the dark and dangerous deeds they would participate in later that night.

Emily was so distracted by her thoughts, she barely noticed Eric and Dane pull her to a stop in the middle of the rink, under the giant mirror ball. But she sure as hell noticed when they both got down on one knee.

"What is happening?" she said, the sudden panic gripping her insides making itself known in the high pitch of her voice.

"Don't worry, kitten, none of us are ready for that question."

"Yet," Dane stressed, casting a sideways glance at his brother.

"Okay, so... what's all this then?"

Eric took a breath then cleared his throat. It felt weird, seeing her strong, stoic man nervous, but when he looked up at her, his gaze held nothing but quiet assuredness. "Emily Berringer, will you be our girlfriend?"

Her eyes widened and her mouth fell open as she stared back at them, her men, and absorbed their very serious question. Then she rolled her eyes and giggled, shook her head with affectionate incredulity. "It's about bloody time."

Chapter Sixteen

E ric felt amazing.

Except for the fact he was about to watch his girlfriend race a criminal at breakneck speeds and there wasn't a thing he could do to stop it. Not if they wanted to get this creep and his little enterprise off the streets.

When they had arrived at the meeting point, it was purposely half an hour late. The first reason being they had wanted to spend as much time with Emily as possible, showing her off to everyone at the roller disco and dispelling her fear they were anything like that arsehole, Billy.

The second reason was the intention of pissing off Shane, but the joke was on them. He hadn't arrived either.

An hour later and they were still waiting.

"Do you think he knows?" Dane murmured, as they pretended to be interested in the purple Lamborghini rolling past them, AC/DC blasting from within.

"How could be know?" Emily asked.

She was safely tucked between him and Dane, looking cute as fuck in her tight blue jeans and a yellow leather jacket that clung to her curves, and was drinking coffee from the servo down the street.

Their *girlfriend*. Officially.

And all of a sudden he felt amazing again.

Until his brother reached over the top of Emily and flicked his forehead. "Get your head in the game."

Eric's gaze connected with Dane's and he realised he was smiling. He couldn't help it. He was happy, giddy even. But Dane was right. *Focus*. "I doubt he knows. More likely, he's playing mind games."

"He wants to piss us off, like we tried to do to him?" Emily said.

"Exactly. But with guys like this, it's also a boost to their ego. By making everyone wait for him he can prove how important he is."

"Wow," Emily drawled. "Tell me you have a small dick without telling me you have a small dick."

Dane chuckled and shook his head. "So you're saying punctuality equals big dick energy?"

"Absolutely."

"You do remember that we also arrived late?" Eric reminded her.

"Yeah, but I've already seen your dicks," Emily said, grinning, "and generally speaking, you two are *very* punctual."

Dane matched her grin. "Have we told you lately how much we love you?"

"Not since you asked me to be your girlfriend," she said, her cheeks colouring with that sweet rosy blush that was all Emily.

Eric bent his head to kiss their girl when an engine revved and a cheer went up through the crowd and the familiar rumble of a Mustang grew closer.

"Show time."

They continued standing beside Dane's car, watching and listening to the goings-on around them. Shane took his time making his way over to them, shaking hands and kissing women and posing for photographs. *Wanker.* Eric even caught a glimpse of Detective Cross amongst the crowd, blending in with the rest of the hoons, drooling over engines and ogling pretty girls.

The local police had been given a heads-up about the race too, and asked to minimise their presence where possible. So far, so good with only one patrol car driving by in the last hour. Which meant they were just waiting on the douchebag with delusions of grandeur to make his move and get this race on the road.

"Um, hello." A trio of young women approached them while they waited.

"What do you want?"

"Don't be rude." Emily scowled up at him, then smiled at the girls. "Sorry about him. He's a grumpy bugger. What's up?"

One of the young ladies glanced cautiously at him and Dane, before speaking to Emily. "Ah, we just wanted to say good luck, and that we hope you win."

"You do?"

"Yeah, of course we do." The older girl in the trio thumbed over her shoulder at the mostly male crowd. "These guys never take us seriously as drivers. It'd be really cool if someone made them change their tune."

Emily's smile lit up the night. "I'll see what I can do," she said, then shook their hands. "Thanks for coming out tonight."

"No probs. Good luck."

"See?" she said, as the girls moved on to the next car.

"No need to be rude. Not everyone at these things is a terrible person."

No. Many of them are victims. But he kept the thought to himself and kissed her temple instead. His sweet girl needed to focus on the race and not the plight of others.

That was his job.

Eventually Shane made his way over to them, his brother and groupies in tow, all of them grinning like idiots. "You showed up."

Emily folded her arms over her chest. "You didn't think I'd come?"

Dane snorted. "He's gunna wish you didn't."

"On the contrary," Shane said, sliding his slimy gaze from the top of Emily's head to the tips of her sneakers and back again, lingering on her breasts. "I love a bitch who comes when I tell her to."

Just like the night before, the crowd made stupid wooing noises in an attempt to keep the smack talk going. And just like the night before, the urge to rip Shane Spencer's throat out had Eric taking a step forwards, but to everyone's surprise, Emily started laughing.

She nudged him and Dane. "What did I tell you?" She tilted her chin at Shane. "Small dick energy."

The young women they'd spoken to earlier burst out laughing, as did several others, including Detective Cross, who had worked his way to the front of the gathering. The laughter eased Eric's tension just enough to stop him from doing anything stupid.

Shane smiled but there was no humour in it. "When it comes to small dicks, I guess you're the expert."

Again Emily shocked him, this time by reaching down and grabbing the front of his jeans. He was already semi-hard just from being in her presence, and would bet good money his brother was too, but feeling her small hand cup his balls before rubbing his shaft through the soft denim sent a spike of arousal to his brain and made his dick as hard as steel.

Then Emily moulded the denim around his cock, showing off his shape and size, and said, "You tell me, ladies, do I look like the *small* dick expert?"

Multiple women leered at Eric and Dane and made appreciative noises, and from the corner of his eye, he saw Detective Cross laugh and take a photo.

Great.

Leaning into her ear, he growled, "Kitten." It was meant as a warning.

One she ignored when she smiled up at him, gave him another squeeze, and whispered, "Just go with it."

Glancing at Dane, Eric shook his head. His brother had folded his arms over his chest and was rocking his hips forwards, blatantly pressing his cock into Emily's grasp while grinning at their prey. Eric cleared his throat to get Dane's attention.

"Yeah, like I'm ever going to tell our girl not to touch my dick." Dane shot him his best "are you stupid?" look. "I mean, come on."

They've both lost their damn minds.

"How about we stop measuring our dicks and get this show on the road," Eric said.

Shane nodded. "Agreed."

"Spoil sport," Emily whispered, then blew a kiss at him.

Catching her chin between his fingers, Eric squeezed, and said, "Don't make me put you over my knee in front of all of these people, kitten." Her eyes immediately widened and her pupils dilated, and he was pretty sure she was about to beg him to fuck her again when Dane tapped his shoulder.

"And you think I'm bad," he said, chuckling. "You look like you're about to throw her over the bonnet and give her a good hard fuck."

"I'd be down for that." She practically sighed the words, and didn't break eye contact for even a second.

One corner of his mouth twitched up. "Only if you're a good girl," he said. "And win the race."

"What if I lose?" She pouted.

"Then prepare for a spanking," he said.

Emily's jaw dropped before she realised he was joking and she rolled her eyes at him. "I'm winning this race," she said, bopping him on the tip of his nose with her finger. "You just watch me."

"Are you done eye-banging your bitch, or what?" Shane said as he approached, then gestured for them to pop the bonnet. "Let's see what you're working with."

It went against every fibre of Eric's being to ignore the shithead's disrespect, but one small shake of Emily's head was enough to cool his temper and get on with the job. He also expected the arsehole to make rude comments about Dane's car—the only other love in his brother's life—but Shane simply grunted and looked vaguely impressed, then invited them to check out his engine.

Dane and Emily obliged while Eric stayed with the car. He didn't trust one of Shane's cronies not to tamper with it and do something that could cost Emily the race.

As it was, Shane seemed far too relaxed for a man about to lose his prized possession. But maybe he truly didn't believe that Emily was any kind of threat to him. It was possible, he supposed. As those girls had said earlier, men always underestimated women when it came to cars. And unlike Eric and Dane, Shane didn't have the advantage of knowing how kickass their woman was on the track. He'd never seen her race before. They had.

With that thought in mind, Eric couldn't help the smile that crept across his face as he watched Shane and Emily interact. She was right. He did give off small dick energy. But wasn't that the problem with every guy that underestimated a woman regarding everything?

He hoped he and Dane were smarter than that, but knew realistically they were going to screw up again. Not that Emily was a perfect human either.

But she was perfect for them.

"Last chance to forfeit, cutie," Shane said, twirling his keys around his finger. "We're talking V8s here. That's a lot of power for a little girl. You sure you can handle it?"

Emily returned to Eric's side, leaned into him and slid her hand over his chest, his heart. Her touch was firm and sure and just a little possessive, and his cock—which had resumed slumbering against his thigh—sprung to attention so fast it made his head spin, but he held himself in check. *Focus, idiot.*

"You should be less concerned about what I can handle," Emily said, "and more concerned with what I'll do to your car when I win." She tapped her finger against her chin. "I wonder how much I can get for those fuck ugly rims?"

"Good thing you'll never need to know." Shane scowled. "Let's race."

Chapter Seventeen

<hr>

D ane helped Emily into the driver's seat and buckled her into the racing harness. "How are you feeling, baby?" When she didn't immediately answer him, he stopped what he was doing and squeezed her thigh. "Emily, look at me."

She lifted her gaze to his and nodded, but her smiled looked forced. "I'm okay. I promise."

"Just remember, you don't have to do this," he said. "If you're having any doubts at all, we can call the whole thing off right now."

As per their meeting with Detectives Bryant and Cross that morning, Dane knew one phone call was all they needed and Hell would descend on the hoons. They also knew that some of them would get away to drag another day, but the main aim of the operation was to scoop up Spencer and his crew, and the drug dealers that always seemed to slither in and take advantage of the extra cover supplied by the crowds and chaos.

He'd be lying if he said he wasn't worried about Emily,

that he would be happy if she changed her mind and called it quits on the race.

What if she got caught up in the action at the end of the night?

What if he and Eric couldn't get to her in time and she got arrested along with everyone else?

What if she crashed?

The sudden heat of her palm on his cheek brought him back from the brink. "It's going to be okay. I'm going to be okay, so stop worrying."

"The day I stop worrying about you is the day I die."

Her whole expression softened and her smile turned kinda goofy. "I love you too."

And he just stayed there, crouched down beside her, basking in her love until his brother called out for him. "Derek, is she ready?"

Dane straightened and dusted his hands off on his jeans. "Are you ready, baby?"

"As ready as I'll ever be," she murmured, then gave him a thumbs-up.

"Just remember what we spoke about on the drive over. You've driven my car before, you know the timing. And you know this road. You drive it almost daily. Trust your reflexes." One corner of his mouth tipped up. "You remember why he calls you kitten, right?"

Emily rolled and eyes and huffed out a laugh. "Because I have the reflexes of a cat."

"Yes, you do."

"You know, I'd prefer to think it's because I'm soft and adorable."

"You're that too." Dane closed the driver's door and leaned in through the open window. "Kick his arse, baby." Then he kissed her deeply.

Until a hand landed on his shoulder. "Move over." A moment later Emily giggled as his brother took his place and kissed her too.

"We'll be waiting for you, kitten."

"You better be," she said, then winked. "I was promised a good hard railing if I win."

Eric growled. Dane chuckled. "That's the plan."

"Good," she said, then started the engine. "You might want to step back."

Stepping away from the car was harder than it should have been. Emily knew what she was doing behind the wheel. Dane knew that, but his instinct to protect his woman was at war with his need to do his duty.

"Come on," Eric said. "Em has it from here." Then he tilted his chin at her. "Come back to us in one piece."

She gave him a nod, then revved the engine, signalling she was ready to race.

Dane and Eric moved to the side and made eye contact with Detective Cross. He scratched his chin. The signal that everything was set.

Good.

The sooner they got this over with, the better.

Shane stood ready to get in his car and addressed the crowd. "You know the race. You know the stakes. If I lose," —a chorus of booing and jeering filled the air—"I forfeit the Coyote. But if I win,"—he stared directly at Dane and Eric —"your bitch is mine. And I'm gunna fuck her up so good, she'll never want to leave me."

Dane took a step forwards but Eric grabbed his shoulder and held him back. They'd done that a lot in the last twenty-four hours. Stopped each other from doing dumb shit like punching people who really deserved it. Sometimes being one of the good guys sucked.

"Never gunna happen, Shane," Eric said. "Our girl is gunna crush you."

Shane's only response was to laugh, then get in his car.

Emily knew the route she had to drive. It was on the note Shane had dropped off that afternoon at the dealership. A three kilometre stretch along Mount Cotton Road, between Ney and Redland Bay Roads. It was a hotspot for illegal drag racing and dangerous as fuck.

Curvy roads through semi-rural land, which meant kangaroos, wallabies and the occasional koala were potential hazards, especially at midnight. Concealed driveways on both sides of the road, not to mention the way the road curved and dipped, and oh, yeah, had single fucking lanes, which meant someone had to drive on the wrong side of the road for this insanity.

But they knew the drill. Shane's crew had the area blocked off. The local residents knew the drill too and tended to steer clear of it all, but there would be at least one call to the local coppers about the hoons in the area. Thankfully the boys in blue had already been informed of what was going on and, barring any other major incidents, were on hand to help with the clean up.

Emily and Shane moved into position, both of them revving their engines and spinning their tyres, leaving rubber on the road for better traction and a cleaner take off.

Dane's heart was in his throat. He didn't want to watch but he couldn't look away. He couldn't let his girl out of his sight.

Even after they took off in a roar of heavy metal and a cloud of burning rubber.

"She can do this," Eric said, then moved off to speak to Detective Cross.

As always, his brother was right. Emily had been racing

cars with her family for years. She'd even raced them. She was amazing. And she was all theirs. A slow grin slipped into place as his pride for his girl made itself known. Emily Berringer was short, curvy, and owned more sass than Dane knew what to do with.

And she was about to beat Shane fucking Spencer at his own game.

He looked over at Matthew Spencer and honestly wondered if he should shake the idiot's hand. If it wasn't for that little twat lying to Emily and bringing her out to an illegal drag race, he and Eric could have lost her for good.

Just as the thought went through his mind, Matthew turned and caught Dane staring at him, grinning at him. "What's so funny?"

"Your brother is about to have his arse handed to him by a little girl. That shit is funny."

Matthew kicked at a stone on the pavement. "He's not going to let her win."

"Well that's a co-inky-dink, because Emily isn't going to let him win either."

"Yeah. Sure." Matthew looked nervous. More than nervous. The kid looked like he needed to vomit.

A pit formed in Dane's gut. Something wasn't right. Grabbing Matthew's upper arm, he jerked him closer and he didn't care who saw it. "Something you want to tell me, mate?" The kid swallowed hard and began to shake his head, but Dane shook him harder. "Don't even think about lying to me. Not if it has something to do with Emily."

Nodding, words began started spilling out of Matthew, like a confession avalanche. And just like an avalanche, it destroyed everything in its path.

"Shane's going to mess her up, he's going to make sure she can't win."

"What do you mean? Explain."

"He's got a guy ready to run her off the road. If it even looks like she might win, he'll make the call and—"

"And what?" Dane snarled, his temper clawing at him like the beast it was. But he couldn't unleash it. Not yet. Not until he had all the information.

"He'll kill her," Matthew said, sweat beading on his brow and upper lip. He shook his head, his eyes wide and haunted. "He'll make it look like an accident, but he'll kill her."

Dane grabbed the kid by his ear and dragged him, literally kicking and screaming over to Eric and Cross. "Tell them," he demanded. "Tell them what you just told me."

Matthew's gaze darted between the three older men as he rubbed at his ear, but he did as Dane demanded and told them what Shane had in store for Emily.

"Fuck," said Cross, then pulled out his phone and pointed a finger at Matthew. "Detain him, and keep him quiet." Then he called in the cavalry.

The kid was in cuffs before he could blink, and he didn't even argue. "I never wanted her to get hurt." He shook his head. "But she humiliated Shane. He was never going to let her win."

Dane stared at his older brother and knew he too felt the pain around his heart, the squeezing sensation that had the power to cripple them where they stood.

With the speeds Emily was doing and the distance they were travelling, at most the race would have taken about a minute and a half, which meant it was already over. And they were close enough to the action that they would have heard a crash. But....

No. No buts. Fuck that.

They weren't giving up.

Not on her.

"She'll be okay. She will," Dane insisted. "Emily is one of the best drivers we've ever known. Our girl will be okay."

Eric nodded. "You're right. She will." Then the sound of mass panic hit their ears as all hell broke loose. "Let's get to work."

The task force swooped in, and with the aid of the local coppers, they managed to arrest several people, either on suspicion of supplying drugs, or a variety of traffic offences. As expected, many of the hoons got away, disappearing into the darkened suburban streets. There was simply too many of them, and not enough police resources to go around.

About ten minutes into the chaos, Detective Cross got a call from Detective Bryant. They had detained Shane and a handful of others at the finish line, but there was no sign of Emily. And investigators further up the road hadn't seen her either. There was no evidence of a crash, no debris. It was as though she had vanished into thin air.

Where could she have gone?

It was almost another ten minutes before Dane heard a familiar engine rumbling and the tightness around his heart eased. His fear subsided and he called out to Eric. "She's here. Our girl is here."

Eric ran over to where Dane stood and together they watched his car come slowly into view, before pulling off to the side of the road. A moment later they were hauling Emily out of the car and checking her over for any injuries.

"I'm fine," she insisted, smiling as they showered her in kisses. "I told you I'd be okay."

"Where the bloody hell have you been?"Dane snapped. "We were worried sick."

Emily's irritation exploded out of her as she tugged off

her gloves. "Some *fuck-knuckle* came flying out of a concealed driveway and I had to make a hard left onto Lyndon Road, and I was going too fast to turn around so I just followed it all the way up. But then I had to cut all the way around Capalaba just so I could loop back up to here. And don't even get me started on the traffic. Doesn't anyone have anything better to do on a Saturday night?"

Neither Dane nor Eric could hold in their laughter any longer. Emily looked so exasperated as she told them about her detour, and they were so relieved that she was truly all right, that she was so completely oblivious to the true danger she'd been in, that they just had to let it out, to let it be known they were happy and no one was going to change that anytime soon.

"I love you, baby," Dane said, pulling her in for a hug.

"I love you, too," she said, snuggling against him.

"And I love you both," Eric said, then kissed the top of Emily's head. "I love our weird little family."

"We're not weird," Emily said, frowning. But when Dane cocked one brow at her, she added, "Okay, so maybe we're a little bit weird."

"And you're okay with weird?"

"Depends. Are you going to take me home so we can have weird sex now?"

Dane shook his head and laughed again. "Who says we're taking you home first?"

Even in the moonlight, he could see her pupils dilate, and he'd bet good money her panties were wet through. "Well, in that case," she purred, "I am *very* okay with it."

And so was Dane.

It had taken a while to find their perfect match, a woman who was open to the idea of sharing herself with two men—two brothers—but Emily was it for them. Dane doubted she'd even had a second thought about the whole idea. That was just the kind of woman she was.

Kind and accepting.

Loving.

Theirs.

Epilogue One

Monday morning rolled around all too fast.

Dane stared at himself in the mirror and wondered not for the first time if he should grow a beard. He was twenty-nine years old but passed for much younger thanks to his boyish good looks. And a beard would add a little extra something to Emily's enjoyment when he went down on her.

She'd made the comment just last night that his stubble felt amazing against her clit.

Unfortunately, he also knew he would earn a look of displeasure from their Aunty Jo should he dare to show up at the station looking less than perfectly groomed, so he picked up his shaver and made himself presentable.

By the time he had finished his morning routine, Eric and Emily were awake and in various stages of their own rituals. The upside to owning a house with two bathrooms was no one had to wait in line. But now that Emily was here, he figured they would need to rethink things. He couldn't deny he had already drawn up some renovation ideas with a bigger bedroom, a more luxurious bathroom, and a walk-in wardrobe.

Anything to make their girl more comfortable.

"You're up early," Eric said, lifting the coffee pot in silent question.

Dane nodded, then slid into a chair at the table. A moment later a pair of feminine arms wrapped around his neck and the subtle scent of Emily's perfume hit him right in the dick. He would swear that perfume had some kind of pheromone booster in it. It was either that, or the simple fact that she was officially in their lives now, that made him want to fuck her brains out every time she came anywhere near him.

Pulling her into his lap, he slid his hand along her inner thigh. She was wrapped up in Eric's bathrobe, her hair still damp, her face fresh and free of makeup, and as his hand explored farther under the robe he discovered she was still delightfully nude.

"Good morning," he murmured against her neck, then pushed her thighs apart and pressed his thumb against her clit. "Are you wet for me, baby?"

Emily swallowed then nodded. "Always."

"Such a good girl," he growled, then slowly slid a finger into her pussy and bit down into the muscle connecting her shoulder and neck.

Her needy moan was music to his ears. And the way her body arched in his lap, the way she wriggled and squirmed and tried to force him to do more than tease her was fucking adorable.

Dane had never been as dominant as Eric, had never felt the need to choke or spank, but he got off on this. He got off on controlling Emily's body, controlling her orgasms and giving her as many as she could take, as many as she would beg for.

"Please, Dane. Please fuck me."

"Tell me how you want it, baby. Give me details."

He knew that was the hard part for her, telling them exactly what she wanted. Emily was so used to being the dutiful daughter, of essentially having her wants and needs ignored in favour of pleasing others, that she had given up on ever getting what *she* wanted out of life, but they were determined to show her she could have anything—*every-thing*—she wanted, if only she could learn to ask for it.

"Don't make me say it," she whined, and wriggled again.

Dane added a second finger and curled them ever so slightly, found that special spot he knew drove her crazy and applied pressure. She tried to close her legs, to pin his hand in place, but then Eric was there, kneeling in front of her and forcing her knees apart.

"Tell Dane what you want, kitten. Let him give you what you need."

Grateful for the assist, he cast his brother a sly smile before focussing 100 percent of his attention back on their girl. "You can do this, baby. Tell me what you want. Whisper it in my ear. Tell me all the dirty, depraved things you fantasise about."

"I can't."

"You can."

Her cheeks pinkened and she ducked her head, diverted her gaze away from them. "It's embarrassing."

Dane chuckled. "This from the woman who demanded a good railing if she won an illegal street race."

Her brow pinched with irritation. "That was different," she said, still wriggling in his lap. "That was the adrenaline talking. And you did rail me, and it was amazing, and I didn't need to,"—she gasped—"provide... details."

Dane bowed his head to hide his smirk. Their girl was so fucking cute when she was riled up and horny. But then Eric stroked her cheek, and said, "It's only us here, Emily." His brother's voice held a soothing note that calmed her. Truth be told, it calmed him too. "You needn't be embarrassed in front of us. Tell Dane what you want him to do. Tease him with details, the way he's teasing you right now."

That got her attention. "Tease him? Is that something guys like?"

"It's something this guy likes," Dane said, and increased the pressure he was applying to her G-spot. She rolled her lips between her teeth but that didn't stop the sexy little whimper from escaping her. "Tease me, baby. Make me work for it."

"I already said I want you to fuck me," she said, her voice so soft and unsure.

"Yes, but *how* do you want me to fuck you? Hard and fast, or slow and deep?"

"Do you want him to make you cry, or do you want to scream his name?"

"I—" She shook her head. Gasped again. "I don't know."

"Yes, you do. We know you, baby. We know you're used to putting yourself second to everyone else. But we've also seen how ferocious you can be. How determined you are." He slid his fingers from her body and raised them to her lips. "Open up."

Emily's pupils were so dilated, Dane could see his own reflection, but she was hesitant to open her mouth.

Until Eric snarled at her. "Now, kitten."

She opened up on a gasp and Dane slid his fingers along her wet, silky tongue. He loved the way her eyelids fluttered as the taste of her pussy hit her, loved hearing her whimper and moan, and understood completely.

One taste of her sweet cunt and he was hooked.

"Tell Dane your secrets, kitten," Eric said, as he slipped free the knot in the belt securing her robe and pulled it open. "It's okay to be selfish sometimes. To put yourself first. Tell him what you want."

Grabbing his wrist, Emily eased Dane's fingers from her mouth and placed his hand on her breast, then gnawed at the corner of her lip. "I want...," she whispered, then took a breath. "I want you to make love to me, slow and deep."

Dane massaged her breast and nuzzled against her neck. "Is that all?"

She shook her head and looked uncertain. "I want you to flip me over and fuck me hard like you did when you took me home after the race. Right here. On the table."

Then she lifted her chin and half glared at them, as if waiting for them to make fun of her. Instead, Dane stood up, taking Emily with him, and sat her on the edge of the table. A flick of his wrist and the towel secured around his waist was on the floor and he was nestled between her thighs, his hard cock jutting up between their bodies.

His brother handed him a condom but before he could tear open the foil packet, Emily placed her hand over his and shook her head again. "Would it be okay if we didn't use that?"

Dane shared a look with Eric, then stared into Emily's eyes and cupped her cheek. "Do you understand what you're asking of us?"

A shy smile decorated her pretty face as she looked from him to Eric and back again. "To make it messy?"

"Messy is one word for it," Eric said, his familiar stoicism blanketing his expression, then he cocked one brow and a slow smile spread across his face making him more sinister than stern. "Or are you hoping to get pregnant? Tell us the truth, kitten. Do you want us to put a baby in you?"

A shiver ran through her even as her eyes widened and her blush returned. "What? No. I'm not ready for that just yet," she said. "I get the contraceptive injections every three months. But you said to tell you what I want, and what I want is to feel you. All of you. Both of you. With nothing between us." She looked away again. "But it's fine... if you don't want to. I get it."

"Of course we want to," Dane said. "We want to give you everything you want."

Placing his hand between her breasts, he pressed her down onto the table. The robe would protect her skin from the timber surface, but nothing would protect her from their obsession. She was their addiction.

Her body, mind and heart were theirs for the keeping.

The look in Emily's eyes as she stared up at him was intoxicating. He'd never known he could love someone so much, want to care for and look after someone so much, yet still want to treat her like his own personal fuck toy.

He slid his hands along her thighs and pushed them wide, then leaned down and laved his tongue against her pussy. Her flavour hit him like too much whiskey, intoxicating yet enticing him to taste a little more, making his insides warm and his body relax. And her moan....

Heavenly.

From the corner of his eye, he saw Eric move to the other side of the table, heard him say to her, "That's it, kitten. That's our good girl." Then the wet sounds of kissing met his ears, making him smile.

Wrapping one arm around her thigh to hold her in place, Dane used his free hand to keep her legs apart while he licked and sucked on her clit, took her to the edge but not quite over it. Not yet. The sounds she made, the way she whimpered and whispered his name, made him want to bury himself deep inside her and never come out.

And he had teased her enough.

Standing up straight, he grabbed Emily around her thighs and moved her so her arse teetered on the very edge of the table, then inch by painstaking inch, he slid his cock deep inside her, gave her exactly what she wanted, let her feel every part of him. And he loved feeling every inch of her, loved taking his time to stroke her skin and bask in the heat of her lusty gaze.

"Dane," she breathed. "Yes."

"Come here, baby." His brother helped their girl to sit up and wrap her arms around Dane's neck, then he started rocking his hips, slowly easing in and out of her tight, wet cunt.

Closing his eyes, he took a moment to enjoy the feel of Emily's core wrapped around his aching cock. Without the condom to dull his senses, he could feel everything. Her slick heat, her silky softness... she felt amazing.

Dane took his time and fucked her good and slow, revelled in the feel of her soft body and even softer moans, until a surge of feeling welled up inside him, a feeling he'd only ever felt for one woman.

Emily.

Releasing her legs, he fisted his hand in her hair and took her mouth with all the passion she inspired in him.

"Fuck, yes." The faint sound of Eric jerking off only fuelled Dane's lust and it was taking every iota of his concentration to stop himself from coming.

Not yet.

Pulling back, he stared at Emily's kiss-swollen lips, was

enthralled by her beautiful eyes, hazy with hunger under half-shuttered lids, and knew he couldn't hold back any longer. He needed to come and he wanted to take her with him.

"Time for hard and fast, baby."

In one fluid movement he pulled out of her pussy, flipped her over and slammed back inside her, her hair still gripped in one hand like a leash while she pushed herself up on her hands and held her body off the table.

Pounding his hips against her, he devoured the sight before him. Her back arched, her voluptuous arse sticking out, bouncing every time he thrust inside her as he kept his promise and fucked her hard and fast. "Fuck, baby. You feel so fucking good."

Reaching under her, he thumbed her clit, applied pressure to the swollen little nub until she began to shiver, until he felt the tell-tale tremors of her muscles contracting around his thick intrusion.

When her body began to convulse and her moans devolved into silent screams, that's when he let himself go. Gripping her fleshy hips in both hands he sealed their bodies together until his cock stopped jerking inside her and his thighs were coated in Emily's wetness. Then he staggered back and practically fell into the chair behind him, his legs so weak they couldn't sustain his weight for one moment more.

But his new seat gave him a premium view of his girl's dripping cunt, of the messiness she'd told them she wanted. A messiness Eric added to as he unloaded his own grunting orgasm onto her pretty pink pussy, before using his fingers to push their combined mess up inside her.

Emily's legs hung limply over the edge of the table, her toes barely touching the floor. Eric helped her sit back in

Dane's lap before demanding she clean their come off his fingers. A command she obeyed much more eagerly than before.

Then she snuggled against him and sighed softly. "I vote for calling in sick and fucking all day. Who's with me?"

Dane chuckled and Eric shook his head, although his brother was still smiling. "No can do, baby. Not with our job."

She nuzzled against his throat and licked the salty sweat that clung to his skin, urging him to reconsider. *Be strong.* "It was worth a shot."

He chuckled again, then slapped her backside. "Up you get. Time for work."

Emily pouted at them one more time, then rolled her eyes when they wouldn't budge. "Fine," she said, standing up. "I need another shower now anyway."

As she walked away, his gaze was glued to her sexy arse until she disappeared into the main bathroom. "*That* was fucking intense," he said.

Eric grinned. "I have a feeling it always will be with her."

"I know it will."

Dane knew in his heart he would never get enough of her.

Their woman.

Their sexy kitten, their sassy baby.

Their sweet Emily.

Epilogue Two

It had been two months since the excitement of her race against Shane Spencer, and Emily was more than happy for her life to go back to its normal, boring self. In fact she almost appreciated it more, now that she'd had a taste of that world. A world her brother had tried to warn her about. One that Eric and Dane were determined to protect her from.

One she was happy to put in her rearview mirror.

When her parents and younger brother had returned home from their respective holidays, she had announced that she was officially dating two men. And not just any men, but her future sister-in-law's brothers.

But apparently she had underestimated exactly how much of a secret their flirting was, as neither her mother nor father seemed surprised by the news, and Easton had simply shrugged and asked if there were any chips in the pantry.

Teddy was still warming up to the idea, especially after watching the security footage of a certain someone making coffee while naked, but he and Eric and Dane had started hanging out more often, usually sharing a few beers while tinkering with one engine or another. And they still made time to visit the track and race each other, and Teddy was still the only person she hadn't beaten.

Yet.

She stared at her brother as she pulled on her racing gloves. "Did Eric and Dane tell you to let me win?"

Teddy feigned ignorance, but Emily wasn't buying it. She cocked one brow and continued staring at him until he caved.

"They may have mentioned something like that. In passing. Possibly. To be honest, I tend to tune out whenever they start speaking."

Emily tried to hold back a laugh and failed. "Teddy, I'm serious."

He shrugged. "So am I."

"Don't you dare let me win just because you feel sorry for me, or you think I *need* this. Because I don't, no matter what those two tell you."

Teddy chuckled and shook his head. "Emmy, since when have I ever let you beat me at anything?"

She frowned and chewed on her bottom lip as she studied her brother. He looked sincere. He *sounded* sincere. But....

"Oh, for fuck's sake," he said, and pulled her into a hug. "If you win today it will be because you're the better driver. Full stop." Then he pushed her back and stared at her like she was an idiot. "Okay?"

Smiling, she nodded. "Okay."

"Good. Let's race."

They made their way over to the cars, playfully shoving each other and laughing as they went. Her brother was sticking with Holden, but instead of a vintage muscle car from their father's stable, he'd opted to put Dane's R8 GTS through its paces.

Emily on the other hand, was driving a BMW M3 Competition sedan, the one she'd acquired from a police auction the previous month and had shipped up from Victoria. And yes, she understood the irony of buying a Beamer after telling her men she didn't even like the brand. But how was she supposed to pass up the opportunity of owing an ex-highway patrol car with more mods than she could poke a stick at?

Of course, she'd spent the last month putting her own personal touches on it, starting with a paint job. No one would ever confuse it for a cop car now, not with its bright canary yellow body and sleek black racing stripes. She'd also modified the exhaust, upgraded the sound system and, for the first time ever, she had given her car a name.

Birdie.

She thought it fitting considering the colour.

She climbed in, strapped in and started the engine. Birdie purred to life. Until Emily hit the accelerator and then she roared. A glance to the sidelines told her Eric and Dane were watching her closely, and for a moment she got distracted, remembering all the things they'd done for her, and to her, in the last few weeks.

Hell, the last few nights.

Emily had spent so much time over at their house, they'd asked her to move in. She wasn't sure she was quite ready for that yet, but she was all in when it came to exploring her newfound sexuality and all the naughty ways her boyfriends expressed their love and appreciation for her. Sometimes she even did things on purpose, like hide their shields, misplace their keys, things she knew would earn her a trip over Eric's knees for a spanking, while Dane force-fed her his cock.

She was so distracted by these thoughts that it was only when her brother honked his horn that she realised she was still staring at Eric and Dane instead of paying attention to the cars.

Giving Teddy a thumbs-up, Emily revved her engine again and laid some rubber on the track before rolling forwards to the starting line and triggering the lights.

After that, the only thought in her head was....

Win.

Emily knew the timing of the lights. She'd had the pattern memorised for years. The only difference between her and her older brother was reaction speed, that was what won races like this.

Her adrenaline was high, her concentration solid, and as she watched those lights flicker downwards without even a second of time between them, her excitement and anticipation sharpened her senses and calmed her mind, and by the time the green light lit up, she was in motion.

Flying down the track like a bat out of Hell.

And it was all over in ten seconds flat.

Emily knew she hadn't won, but she couldn't deny it was a rush.

Slowing her car down, she took the slip road to cut back around to the pre-staging area, and petted her steering wheel. "Good girl, Birdie. We'll get him one day."

But as she turned the corner, she saw her family waving and jumping up and down, screaming incomprehensible things. She parked her car, then realised Teddy was pulling up behind her.

What was going on?

Suddenly Eric and Dane were there, pulling her free

from the driver's seat and kissing her as though they hadn't seen her in a year.

"You won!" her mother screamed. "I'm so proud of you, Emmy. You won."

"What?" A loud rushing sound filled Emily's ears and she shook her head, sure she'd misheard her mother. "I don't think—"

But then she looked over at her brother, who had the biggest grin on his face even as he was casually pulling his leather gloves off. "You beat me, kiddo. Fair and square."

"I did?"

"She's in shock."

"Come here, kitten." Eric pulled her into his arms and held her tightly against his chest, while Dane slid his arms around her from behind. Her men. Her lovers. Her protectors. Always there, always surrounding her with their warmth and their kindness and their love.

"You won, baby," Dane murmured against her ear.

"I know," she said, her voice muffled by Eric's shirt. "I won the night I met you. I won again two months ago, when I started the night with one wrong man, but finished it with two right ones."

Eric pushed her back a little bit, smoothed his hands over her face, and pushed her hair away from her eyes. She stared up at him, saw the worry etched across his features, heard the quiet hitch in his deep voice. "And you're sure you'll be okay with all of this in the long run? The three of us together? It's not always going to be easy. Not everyone will accept our way of life."

Emily looked at the people surrounding them, their families and friends. Everyone who mattered to her was there, celebrating her win, celebrating them. Not a single one of them gave a flying fuck about her sex life.

"I'm sure," she said with a smile. "Just like I'm sure I'll need a key."

Eric frowned. "A key?"

But Dane was already pulling his car keys out of his pocket and sorting through the bunch. "Here," he said, and handed her a newly minted house key. "I had it made in case you changed your mind."

"Consider it changed," she said, then kissed each of her men in turn. "I love you both so much. I just want to be where you are. Always."

Dane grinned. "You realise this means you're stuck with us now?"

"Promise?" There it was again, that hope in her voice. The hope that only her men knew how to elicit.

Surrounding her again, they held her, kissed her. Loved her. "We promise. Always."

I hope you enjoyed Eric, Emily and Dane's story.

Please consider sharing the love by leaving a review for *The Drag Race Debutante and The Detectives* for other readers to find. It doesn't need to be long, and every review is greatly appreciated.

#sharethelove

Prologue

"What in the actual fuck...?"

Lottie Cassidy stared in disbelief at the anonymous email filling the screen of her laptop, a cocktail of confusion, horror and simmering fury filling her belly with lead and causing a cold sweat to sweep over her skin.

And then she opened the attachments.

Just as the email had warned, several photographs of her boyfriend screwing other women appeared, time-stamped and dated. The lead in her belly solidified, the weight of it threatening to crush her.

They'd celebrated their one year anniversary less than a month earlier, and yet there she sat staring at photos of Nate Bellows balls deep in a woman that wasn't her. Two days ago. While he was out of state.

"Good morning, my little goddess."

Nate appeared in the doorway of her bedroom, his sleep-ruffled hair, five o'clock shadow and lopsided grin giving him that rakish look she adored. He had arrived on her doorstep at ten o'clock the night before, looking travel worn and tired after his trip, but not *that* tired, he had assured her as he'd guided her into the shower and banged her against the wall in a passionate quickie, then folded her in his arms as they had crawled into bed.

Now she stared at him over the rim of her computer, a rush of anger making her whole body tremble as she watched him go about his daily morning rituals, as if it was just another day. As if he were a faithful and loving partner, and not a lying, cheating arsehole.

"Are you hungry?" Nate called over his shoulder.

Lottie forced herself to answer, to maintain her calm demeanour as her brain fought to understand what the hell was going on. "No. I've lost my appetite."

Putting down the bacon and eggs he'd pulled from the fridge, he gave her his full attention. "Hey, are you okay?"

Staring at him, at the openness of his posture and the worry etched into his expression, made her breath catch in her lungs and bile swirl in her gut. He looked so sincere, so concerned for her wellbeing. But how could he be? How could he stand there and pretend so artfully to care for her when she'd seen the evidence that it was all a lie?

Her gaze flicked back to her laptop, to the cornucopia of pornographic images splashed across the screen, and that lump of lead in her belly reformed into something sharp and pointed, something dangerous. The sensation caused her to sit very still and rigid, as if one wrong move would pierce her flesh and cut her to shreds.

"I'm fine," she said, offering him a serene smile as she held his gaze, then picked up her phone and called Luke Hardcastle, CEO of Hardcastle Construction and overprotective big brother extraordinaire. The second her brother answered she said, "Fire up the cement truck."

"Fuck. I'm on my way."

At the reminder of her brother's thinly veiled threat to make Nate disappear should he ever dare to hurt her, the concern fell from his face. In its place formed a mask of deadly calm, but under that mask she saw the colour drain away, leaving his perfectly tanned complection looking pallid and weak.

Holding his gaze, she spun her computer around and let him see the fuck-a-thon she'd been subjected to. His jaw tightened, his eyes narrowed and his face reddened so damn fast that if he'd been a cartoon character, she would have sworn the top of his head would have blown off and steam would have shot out his ears.

"Where did you get those?" His voice was so low she barely heard him. The growly masculine baritone she'd come to love, that just last night had made her knees weak and her pussy wet, now made her nauseous.

"It doesn't matter where they came from," she said, her rage springing her from her seat so fast she knocked it over backwards. "Your reaction to them was all I needed to see to know they're real." She shook her head and tried to ignore the prickle of tears threatening to fall, threatening to expose her as weak and emotional.

She would not cry in front of him. She would not give him the satisfaction of watching her heart break.

"Lottie, baby, it's not what you think."

A small disbelieving laugh escaped her. "Not what I think?" She leaned over the laptop screen and pointed to a photograph of Nate and some random woman doing it doggy-style. "So this is you, what...? Helping her find her keys?" She pointed to another photo, another woman. Reverse cowgirl. "What about this one? Pilates?" She made herself look again and nodded. "Definitely Pilates."

"Lottie—"

"Oh, this one is my favourite," she said, cutting him off and pointing to a photo of a blonde woman licking what appeared to be whipped cream off his dick. "And what's going on here, Nate? Feeding the homeless?"

Nate folded his arms across his chest and ran his tongue over his teeth in a show of annoyance. "Okay, now you're just being childish."

"Get out."

"No."

"Get. Out," she said again, this time through gritted teeth. "Now."

"Not until we talk about this."

"We have nothing to talk about. You cheated on me." She slapped her palm against the laptop screen, the evidence there for all to see. "Repeatedly. With multiple women."

"Lottie, I swear to you—"

Straightening to her full height, she anchored her hands to her hips. "How long has this been going on?" she demanded, then another more horrifying thought struck her. "Did you use protection with these women?"

Lottie was a cancer survivor, immunocompromised. She couldn't afford to get some random infection from some random side-chick her boyfriend—*ex*-boyfriend—hooked up with. But when his jaw clenched and his eyes narrowed, she had the answers she needed. "You need to leave."

Before her eyes, Nate's whole demeanour changed. His jaw and shoulders relaxed, he closed his eyes and sighed. "Don't do this," he whispered, opening his eyes again and staring at her like she was his world.

But she wasn't fooled. Not anymore. "I'm not doing anything," she said. "*You* did this, not me. I will not be blamed for *your* shitty behaviour."

"And what shitty behaviour is that, exactly?"

Lottie turned at the sound of her brother's dark voice, and the tightness in her chest eased just a little. The upside to living in the same building as him was that he could be at her door in five minutes flat. Which was useful when the man who'd cheated on her was refusing to leave her apartment.

"How the hell did you get in?" Nate snarled.

Luke held up the spare door key, dangling from his finger. "Now, why doesn't someone tell me why I had to use it."

Nate folded his arms over his chest again and lifted his chin. "This is a private matter between me and your sister. It's none of your business."

Luke's eyes narrowed. "Lottie?" He turned to face her, and she in turn spun the laptop screen in his direction.

Her brother didn't lose his temper often, but when he did, it was spectacular, so she was surprised to see him step quietly towards the table and pick up the computer, stare at the images filling the screen for a minute then softly shut the lid and put it down again.

"Lottie, would you please pack up Nate's things," he said, his demeanour calm, almost mellow. Fatherhood had softened him. "I need to have a word with your ex."

"Ex?" Nate scoffed. "Isn't that for Lottie to decide?"

"She did decide," Luke said, straightening to his full six feet and four inches in height, and folding his arms across his wide chest, mimicking Nate's stance. "The second she called me."

Lottie backed away towards the bedroom. She needed to collect Nate's stuff—which thankfully wasn't much—but she didn't want to miss whatever Luke was about to do to him. It wasn't the first time she'd had to call on her big brother's intimidation tactics. Tactics she'd hoped would never be needed where Nate was concerned.

He was supposed to be different.

He was supposed to love her.

But as she stood there watching him argue with Luke, hearing him admit to the dispicable things he'd done with other women during their so-called relationship, she realised something that sent a chill up her spine and the words were out of her mouth before she could think better of it. Before she could ask herself if she really wanted to know the answer to her heinous question.

"You only wanted me for my money, didn't you?"

She hated the vulnerability in her voice, hated the way her hands shook as she awaited his answer.

Hated feeling weak.

Nate's gaze raked down her body in a way he'd done many times before. Previously, it had made her feel sexy, wanted, alive. Now it made her need a scalding hot shower to wash away the grimy feeling he left on her skin.

"Not at first. You are, after all, a very beautiful woman." He paused and took a step closer. Luke moved to intercede but Lottie touched his arm and halted her brother. She wanted to look Nate in the eye for whatever came next. "But you were also lonely, rich, and... dying."

"You sonofabitch," Luke snarled, but before he could take a swing at Nate, Lottie's fist was flying through the air.

Pain shot through her arm as her small hand connected with her boyfriend's jaw. It felt like punching a brick wall. "Ow!" Immediately, she pulled back and cradled her hand to her chest, glaring at the object of her hatred as she did.

Nate rubbed one side of his jaw, looking more annoyed than hurt. "Really?"

"Get dressed and get the fuck out of here. Now," Luke

snarled at him, then turned his attention to her busted hand. "Let me see it," he said, gently inspecting her fingers.

Nate finally disappeared into the bedroom, resurfacing a few minutes later looking like his usual devastatingly handsome self in jeans and a T-shirt, a duffle bag slung over his shoulder. He stood by the door, one hand on the knob and stared at her, his gaze hot and full of an emotion she couldn't quite identify. "Are you sure you want this, Lottie?"

"Don't engage," Luke whispered. "Just let him leave."

But she never was one for following orders. "Want what?"

The unknown emotion in Nate's gaze solidified in to something she never thought she'd see from him. Pity. "To be all alone again," he said, the soothing timbre of his voice grating on the last of her nerves.

Fury shot though her blood like lightning, heating her up until her skin practically glowed with the emotion. "Better to be alone than stuck with a cheating piece of shit like you."

He opened the door and shook his head, ran his tongue over his teeth. "You think you're so smart, Lottie, but you know as well as I do, you'll never be anything to anyone but a blank cheque and a bony piece of arse."

And then he was gone.

The door slammed shut and she was left alone with her brother and possibly a broken hand.

"I'm taking you to the emergency room. This needs an x-ray."

Lottie nodded, the icy shock of Nate's parting barbs sinking deep into her heart. "Okay," she said, her own voice now oddly emotionless. Her anger had died a swift death, suffocated by the numbness that now held her rigid, afraid to move in case her legs collapsed beneath her.

"Hey." Luke smiled down at her in that same way he always had. The same indulgent smile he now used on his baby son. "I'm proud of you. You've got this. Okay?"

She nodded again, then lifted her chin and forced herself to smile. Luke was right. She had this. She was Charlotte fucking Cassidy. She was a force to be reckoned with.

She'd survived cancer, for fuck's sake. Twice!

She'd survive this too.

Even if it killed her.

More from Jennie Kew

The Bennett's Bastards Series

Third Time Lucky

This Time Around

His Own Heaven

The Viking Blues

Size Doesn't Matter

Glass Half Broken (TBA)

Never The Groom (TBA)

The Brisbane Bachelors Series

The Book Shop Girl and The Billionaire

The Roller Derby Darling and The Delinquent

The Drag Race Debutante and The Detectives

The Boss Babe CEO and The Scoundrel (TBA)

Audiobooks

The Book Shop Girl and The Billionaire

The Q Collection

No Rest For The Wicked

I Saw, I Conquered, I Came

Pushing Rope

Dirty Laundry

Santa Claus Is Coming

Carved In Stone

Battery Operated Boyfriend

Tying The Knot

Quirky: The Complete Q Collection

CERTIFIED 100% SMUT

A Night of Lust and Sexting

Acknowledgements

To my family for all their encouragement, their love and understanding, thank you for being you and for putting up with me being me, especially when deadlines are involved.

And to my readers, thank you for taking this journey with me, and for allowing me to share with you all the people and places who occupy my head and my heart. I hope you enjoy reading about them as much as I enjoy writing about them.

A very big thank you to Rebecca Bavister for her help, and for answering all of my many questions regarding the minutia of day to day life in the Australian Police Service. Also to Sofia Aves for her encouragement and expertise in general motoring knowledge. Your patience, kindness and friendship has been much appreciated these many years.

Meet the Author

Jennie has always enjoyed reading but never had aspirations of becoming a published author. At least not until a dance with death made her ask herself what she really wanted out of life, and she's been writing ever since.

When not writing stories about her imaginary friends, Jennie can usually be found reading a book, watching a movie or building stuff out of Lego. She lives in regional New South Wales with her husband, her husband's magnificent beard, and their small menagerie of furry companions.

www.jenniekew.com

Glossary

As all of my books are set in Australia and use a lot of Australian terms and slang, I've created this guide for my readers to keep you on track when you come across any Aussie-isms in my books.

A bit of all right: If someone is 'a bit of all right' they're considered to be very attractive.

Ambo: Short for ambulance, the term has come to mean anyone associated with any of the public or private ambulance services, their drivers and paramedics.

Arse: Aussie spelling of ass, aka buttocks, bottom, booty and bum.

Arvo and *Sarvo*: 'Afternoon' and 'this afternoon'.

Bonnet and *Boot* (*in relation to cars*): Hood and trunk.

Co-inky-dink: Coincidence.

Copper: Police, cops.

Fashion Rag/Local Rag: Fashion magazine, any locally produced magazines or newspapers.

Fierie/s: Firefighter/s.

Fuck-knuckle: An idiot.

G'day: Pronounced 'gidday', this official Australian greeting is a contraction of the words 'good' and 'day'.

Kiwi: Pronounced 'kee-wee', anyone born in New Zealand.

Larrikin: An unruly, boisterous but generally good natured person, usually male.

Mate: Unlike paranormal or sci-fi erotic romances where your 'mate' is the person you're fated to be with for the rest of your life, in Australian culture 'mate' could mean anyone from your best friend to some random bloke you just met.

Pash/pashing: A passionate kiss.

Pav: Pavlova, a dessert made from baked meringue, topped with cream and fresh fruit, particularly popular around Christmas. We nicked it from the Kiwis.

Phwoar: An estimation of the sound one makes when a bit of all right enters your vicinity. See also, 'panting' and 'drooling'.

RFS: Rural Fire Service.

Sanga: Sandwich.

Servo: a petrol station or service station.

She'll be right, mate: Usually given as a response when someone is offering aid of some kind, it means 'Everything will be fine but thanks for asking'.

Togs: A swimsuit.

Tradie: Any tradesman.

Uni: Pronounced 'you-nee', University aka College.

Yeah, nah and *Nah, yeah*: Whichever word the phrase ends on, is the affirmative answer, therefore 'Yeah, nah' means 'No', and 'Nah, yeah' means 'Yes'.